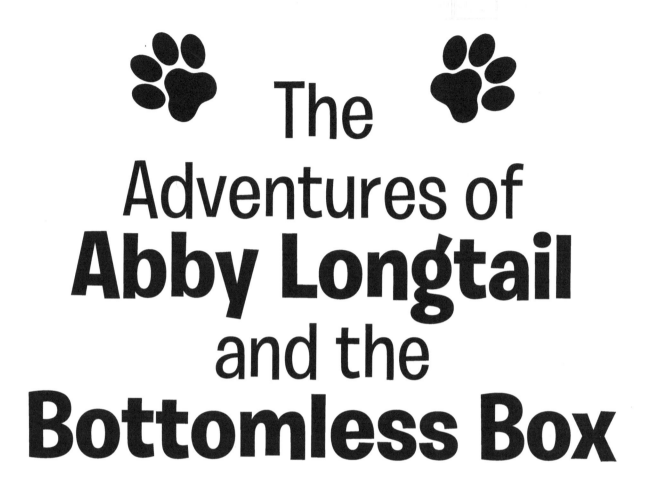

The
Adventures of
Abby Longtail
and the
Bottomless Box

Shirley M. Young

PAGE PUBLISHING, INC.
Conneaut Lake, PA

First originally published by Page Publishing 2021

ISBN 978-1-64701-520-6 (pbk)
ISBN 978-1-64701-521-3 (digital)

Printed in the United States of America

Dedication

To the 2018-2019 4th grade class at St Francis De Sales School, I dedicate this story to show my appreciation for all of the encouragement that you gave me to submit this story to be published. Special thanks go to Connor T., Ellanor S., Reese Z., Joe N., Connor A., Parker S., Matt C., Rex C., Andre B., Kinley D., Lily K., and their teacher Miss A. Tuttle. You touched my heart deeper than I can say, and I will always treasure the support you gave and continue to give. I thank you.

Chapter 1

Abby opened her eyes and looked around. She had been napping in the Mr.'s recliner—one of her favorite places to sleep. Standing, she stretched, first arching her back, followed by each hind leg, one at a time, reaching toward the back of the chair. She finished her warm-up by doing her version of the yoga position *downward dog*. Today was Monday, and it was a very special day. It was the first day that Abby would be alone in the house since she and her family moved in the week before. Abby had her birthday just before the family had moved, and she wanted to do something new, something that she had never done before now that she was a year old. She was no longer a kitten but a grown-up cat.

Abby walked to the kitchen, where the Mrs. was opening a can of her favorite cat food, and watched as the lady spooned it into a pretty crystal bowl. The Mrs. placed the bowl on the floor for the beautiful tuxedo cat—mostly all black, with white around her nose and down into her chest. The Mrs. and the Mr. sat down at the table for their breakfast before leaving for work. Abby overheard the Mr. asking the Mrs. if she thought Abby would be lonesome all day while they were gone. The Mrs. said that she had been wondering the same thing. The Mr. replied that maybe they should think about getting her a playmate. The Lady looked down at their silky black cat enjoying her pâté and smiled, thinking about extending their family with a friend for Abby. After breakfast, the Mrs. and Mr. put on their coats as they were leaving for work. They petted their girl and told her that they would be home at suppertime. They told her that they would miss her but they wouldn't be gone too long, then they went out the door.

Abby ran to the living room and jumped up on the back of the sofa to look out the window. From there, she watched the Mr. and Mrs. as they drove the car out of the garage and left for the day. Once they were out of sight, Abby hopped down and looked around the room. The new house was rather large. There were three floors to roam. The basement was a catchall of sorts with canned goods, exercise equipment, the laundry machines, and Abby's litter boxes. The living room, kitchen, den, and bathroom were on the main floor; and a carpeted flight of steps went to the upstairs, which had bedrooms and a second bathroom. Above the upstairs was an attic, which was an out of the way space under the pitch of the roof. Abby had heard her family talking about storing things in the attic, but she had never been up there. She remembered having a dream the night before that the storage room at the top of the house would be filled with new adventures. The door to the attic was upstairs in the spare bedroom. Would the attic be the place that she would investigate today? Abby wanted the adventure to be something that she would never forget. She thought about the other rooms in the house that she could explore, like the den or the basement, but the attic seemed to call to her, and since it was at the top of the house, Abby reasoned that maybe it would be a top-notch adventure!

The black cat padded up the carpeted stairs, down the hall, and into the spare bedroom. The entrance to the attic was hidden by a full-length mirror that was attached to the attic door. Luckily, the door to the attic was on a magnetic latch. Abby only had to push on the mirror and the latch on the door would release. She pressed her paw on the mirror corner and heard the *pop* of the release and stepped back as the door slowly swung open. Abby cautiously stepped passed the mirror. She saw some wooden stairs that went up to the storage space. A ray of natural light was shining on the flight of steps to guide her way. There must be a window up there, she thought. The cat was anxious and excited as she started her ascent. Up, up, up slowly she climbed the steps that led her to the attic floor. The black cat saw a large room with a bunch of plastic totes, taped-up cardboard boxes marked with black letters, and a couple of metal racks where the Mr. or Mrs. had their winter coats, snow pants, and other outdoor garments.

Abby was disappointed as she looked around. The walls were steeply angled inward and met at the top, making the peak of the house. They were lined with insulation, and the floor was wooden and bare. She stepped into the spacious area and looked around. She had hoped this would be a room full of things left by the previous owners, things to search through and toys to play with. The light from the window shone through enough to let Abby see that everything in the attic was familiar. The containers were some that Mr. and Mrs. brought when they moved to this house. There was nothing new. She decided to walk up and down the length of each wall. Maybe she would find a bug or a mouse that would entertain her. As Abby walked along the far wall, she saw a cardboard box that had been hidden by the shadows of the peaked walls. She was as far from the stairs as she could be in this big room. A spark of hope tickled Abby's belly as she approached the plain cardboard box. It had no markings, and it was not taped shut. She knew she had never seen this box before. The flaps were simply lying on top of one another, almost begging to be opened.

The black cat made her approach cautiously, and then she smelled the box, her long tail twitching with excitement. She walked all the way around the cardboard square. Then, with a deep breath, she reached for the top flap and pulled it toward

her. She unfolded the remaining three flaps away from the opening and looked inside. Although the box appeared to be empty, Abby couldn't see the bottom. She thought that it must be a blanket or a board that was very brown or black. Cats are curious animals, and they love to hop into containers, bags, and boxes. Abby was no different, and she leaped into the box to see what was lining the bottom.

Abby was surprised because she didn't land when she expected. She was falling slowly, as if she were floating, through a tunnel of darkness. The bottom of the box wasn't really a bottom but a portal to another place. Abby barely had time to think about what was happening before she gently landed on her feet in a puff of smoke that twinkled with stars. It was a very soft arrival into a new place. Abby wondered if she was in the basement of the house, since she fell from the attic. She popped her head out of the box and looked around, and she knew right away that this couldn't be their basement. The cat could hardly believe what she saw in front of her. She was sitting in the shade under a big tree, with soft grass all around her cardboard carriage. Not far off she saw a wire fence. Through the fence she could see a Ferris wheel, a merry-go-round, and clowns with balloons. There was also a roller coaster and a waterslide—all under a bright blue sky.

Suddenly, Abby realized that she was outside, and a sense of fear took over. "Outside" was such a big place, and when at home, she didn't go outside. She feared she would get lost and never get back into her warm, cozy home. Once, when she was a little kitten, she had slid past the Mr.'s legs through the door and ran out on the grass. Within seconds she heard a loud yapping sound and found out what a dog was—and she quickly learned that dogs like to chase things that move, just like cats do. The neighbor's dog barked and barked while it chased the young kitten up a nearby tree. When the Mr. rescued the frightened cat, he told Abby that the dog was simply trying to play, but Abby didn't think it was any fun. At that moment, she had decided that she wanted to stay in the house all the time. Now here she was, outside, under a tree. Her reaction was to duck back down in the box and try to return home. She was out of sight but not going anywhere. She peeked out of the box again and looked around. She didn't see any dogs, or anything else that frightened her. Abby sensed a feeling of calmness and felt confident that she was in a safe place.

Cautiously, Abby stepped out of the cushioned travel box and viewed her surroundings. When she looked behind her, she noticed a very large gray-and-black-striped cat lying in the grass. When their eyes met, the striped cat moved into a sitting position. Abby hoped the cat would be friendly and might be able to tell her how to get back home. She started to approach the seated kitty. The cat smiled at Abby and rose to meet her. In a rather-deep voice, the striped cat said, "Good morning and welcome to the carnival. My name is Tiger. You must be Abby."

Abby stopped short, shocked that the big cat knew her name. "Hello," Abby said. "How did you know my name?"

Tiger said, "I had a dream last night, and in my dream a voice told me to come here and that I would meet a black cat with a very long tail and her name would be Abby. My family's home is just around the corner from here, so I decided to see if my dream would come true, and here you are!" Then Tiger said, "My family always talks about going to the carnival, so I had a good idea about what it would be like, but it is even better to see it for myself."

Abby nodded. She said, "I had a dream too. My dream told me to go to our attic, where I would have adventures. After I woke up, I went to the attic and found this box." Abby pointed to the square of cardboard under the tree. "I jumped in the box, and it brought me here."

Tiger said, "That is so exciting! You are so lucky to be able to travel through a box."

Abby cocked her head as she took it all in, whispering, "Doesn't this happen to all cats?"

Tiger shook his head no. "I have a lot of cat friends in my neighborhood, and none of them have ever told me that they have done anything like this."

Abby nodded. "I am lucky. This is really special."

Tiger stuck his paw out for Abby to shake, and Abby met his paw with her own. "It is good to meet you," said Tiger. "Do you want to go to the carnival and see what kind of memories we can make today?"

"Okay!" Abby responded with enthusiasm. "I have never been to a carnival. What kinds of things can we do?"

Tiger pointed toward the entrance then replied, "We can go on fun rides and have yummy carnival treats."

Abby said, "That sounds good. Let's go," and the cats headed into the carnival through the open gate.

Abby stopped to look back at the box that had brought her to this mystical place, then hurried to catch up with Tiger.

They walked toward the merry-go-round, which had ceramic zoo animals with saddles to sit on as the ride went around and around as cheerful carnival music played overhead. When Abby and Tiger got close to the merry-go-round, the ride began to slow down, then came to a stop. Tiger looked at Abby and said, "Hop on!" and the black cat nodded in agreement.

"Which animal are you going to sit on?" asked Abby.

As they stepped onto the base of the ride, Tiger replied, "I pick the elephant," and leaped up on the big gray elephant with long white tusks. Tiger got positioned on the saddle as Abby watched. Tiger returned the question to Abby and asked what her choice would be.

Abby looked around and saw a beautiful zebra with black-and-white stripes. The zebra was positioned exactly halfway around the merry-go-round from Tiger and the elephant. She walked toward the striped zebra and jumped up. "I am going to ride this one because I like the colors!" Once the long-tailed cat was in position on the saddle, the carousel started going in circles while the ceramic animals bobbed up and down on the decorative poles that held them in place.

Speaking loudly so she could hear him over the music, Tiger asked Abby if she was enjoying her ride. Abby smiled at her new friend and nodded. Then Tiger shouted, "After we get off the merry-go-round, we can go to the refreshment stand for a saucer of milk!"

Abby smiled and giggled as the ride went round and round, up and down. The breeze was blowing through her fur, and Tiger was laughing and having fun too. Abby used her long tail to help her keep her balance. *What a wonderful adventure!* she thought. She never would have dreamed it would be anything like this.

After a little while, the merry-go-round slowed down, then stopped, and the cats jumped off. They looked toward a display stand full of snacks made just for a cat's taste buds. Tiger said to Abby, "Come along, my friend. Let's get a snack." There was fresh cream or water to drink and tasty morsels of red meat and fresh fish to eat. For those looking for a snack, a variety of kitty treats were available—just like her Mr. and Mrs. would give to her. Tiger said he was famished, but Abby was more anxious than hungry. The long-tailed cat opted for a little cream and then some water, while Tiger chose something a little more hardy, having fish and water. Off to the side of the refreshment stand was a display of cotton candy. There were swirls of the sweet treat in red, orange, yellow, green, blue, and purple, and the display looked like a fluffy rainbow.

Tiger was giving the cotton candy a good look, and Abby asked her new friend, "Are you thinking about a little dessert?"

Tiger winked and said, "I think I am. That rainbow looks mighty tasty!"

Abby replied with a smile, "It sure couldn't hurt to try it." With that, the two felines each got a cat-size cotton-candy swirl on a stick and licked them clean.

Tiger whispered to Abby that he had been right—it was yummy.

Abby asked, "Shall we go on another ride now and then see what else is here at the carnival?"

Tiger agreed. They had been sitting still for much too long, and there were many things to see and do. The pair went deeper into the carnival grounds, both taking in all the sights and sounds.

It was a small fun-filled park with plenty to keep the two cats happy for the day. The Ferris wheel was the closest ride to them, and they headed straight for it. Without speaking, each cat took a seat and got strapped in. A machine started to move the wheel, and Abby felt a sudden panic of being high off the ground, but then remembered the strap that held her secure, and she relaxed. The big circle began to move, taking the riders up and around, down and around. When the cats were at the top of the wheel, they could look out and see the other rides that were there. They saw the merry-go-round and the refreshment stand, plus bumper cars, a fun slide, and a roller coaster. Near the back fence they saw a rock climbing wall, and next to it was a mechanical bull. The big wheel rolled slower and slower. When it wasn't moving anymore, the furry friends jumped off and ventured on.

The cats went together to the slippery slide, due to Abby's encouragement. It looked like it would be a great deal of fun. There was a steep stairway to climb to get to the top of the slide. Once there, each cat was given a rug to sit on, which would add speed and balance as they rode to the bottom of the stainless steel slope. Cats are known for always landing on their feet, but that didn't happen on this ride! They went down the slide several times, and they would land on their bellies, backs, or on top of each other, laughing all the way. They had deep belly laughs as these two felines became fast friends. They climbed the steps to the slide again and again, each time zooming down the man-made metal mountain to a soft landing area. They sat together on one rug for the last slide, and they landed together in a heap of giggling fur. Tiger was on the bottom of the heap, and between his bouts of laughter, he asked Abby if she was ready to move on.

Still laughing, the cats went to the bumper cars, which were set up just past the slide. They looked at a dozen bumper cars, all different shapes and colors. Abby and Tiger donned racing helmets and then got into the vehicle of their choice. Tiger, a big striped male, got into a car that looked like a tank. Abby found a sleek black hot rod that looked like it could zip around very fast! The friends had a large shaded area to drive around in. The surface was smooth, and the fence enclosing the ride was padded for cushioned collisions. This ride was as much fun as the others had been, and the cats drove around, going fast and spinning in circles while trying to avoid being tagged by others. They were having a wonderful time.

Suddenly, the lights in the canopy over the track started to flash on and off. A buzzer sounded loudly, making the kitties stop their cars and look around, unsure of what was causing the commotion. The buzzer stopped, and a deep voice came over the loudspeaker in the fairground. "Attention, carnival friends! The park will be closing in thirty minutes. Please enjoy one more ride and have a treat from the concession stand before you head for home. Thank you for coming, and please come again soon!"

The new friends climbed out of their bumper cars and came together outside the ride. Abby and Tiger realized their day was drawing to a close, and although they were tired, neither was sure they wanted it to come to an end. The duo was quiet as they each gave thought to what had happened today. Tiger spoke up when he noticed some sadness on Abby's face.

"Abby," he said, "what's wrong?"

Abby looked up when she heard her name. She quietly spoke. "Our day was so much fun. I will miss you."

Tiger gave her words some thought. "I will miss you too, but who knows? Maybe we will do this again. No one knows what the future holds, but I do know that in my near future is a catnap—I'm dog-tired!" Both cats laughed at Tiger's premonition.

Suddenly, the buzzer sounded again, followed by the loudspeaker voice reporting to all, "Attention, carnival friends! The gates to the park will be closed in five minutes. Please exit the facility immediately and come back soon." The buzzer had startled the cats, but they quickly calmed down and headed for the tree that shaded the bottomless box.

When the cats arrived at their destination, Abby was relieved to see that her transportation was still there. She stepped up to the box's edge. She looked at Tiger and asked, "What if it doesn't work? What if I can't go home?"

Tiger placed a comforting paw on Abby's back and said, "Don't worry. You are a very special cat. Whatever made you come here should be able to make you go back. Besides, all cats have a special intuition to go home where they feel safe. We don't think about it, we just know. You coming to the box is a good sign."

The long-tailed cat said, "Thank you, Tiger. That makes me feel better."

Tiger nuzzled close to give Abby a special goodbye. Abby looked up with moist eyes and licked Tiger's forehead as a sign of affection. He purred as she licked his head, then said, "We can always look back to our memories of today, and maybe we will meet again!"

Abby grinned and said, "That would be great!" The black cat took a few steps until she was next to the box. The flaps were folded in on the box, and she used her white-tipped paw to pull back the flaps, just like before.

Tiger came over and looked in. "Hmmm," he said, "it looks just like a regular box to me."

Abby nodded and then replied, "That is just how it looked to me when I jumped in and ended up here. Let's see if it will take me home."

Tiger nodded, and Abby patted Tiger's shoulder. She gave her new friend a wink. She said, "Until we meet again!" and jumped into the box.

Abby woke up on the couch in the living room of her home. The long-tailed cat looked out the window and saw that the sun was on the other side of the sky, which meant the Mr. and Mrs. should be home soon. The memories of the day came flooding in, and Abby realized she didn't remember arriving in the attic, coming down the stairs, or going to sleep. In fact, she didn't remember anything about the return trip that brought her back to her family, except for when she was under the tree with Tiger and she jumped into the box. Now she began to wonder if it all had been a dream. She hopped off the couch and began to investigate, searching for some type of clue to prove that her day had really happened like she remembered it. The black cat ran up the stairs, into the spare bedroom that had the mirror with the magnetic latch. She knew that she wanted to go back to the attic and see if the magical box was real, and if there was any sign of her trip to the carnival and her friend Tiger. Abby lifted her right paw to press on the corner of the mirror to release the door that led to the attic stairs. When her paw was in the air, the cat noticed a sweet-smelling fragrance that made her stop moving. She put her paw down while she sniffed the air, but the aroma was gone. She lifted her paw again toward the door. When she did this, she was able to smell the scent again—and she smiled with recognition. The smell was coming from a little bit of cotton candy that was stuck to the hair around the pads of her soft paw. Abby sat back and brought her paw to her nose, taking in a deep, long breath. Now she was sure that the day had really happened and she had been a part of something very special.

She lay down on the soft carpet and licked away the sweet, special scent on her fur. She knew she would treasure the memory of the amazing day at the carnival, and then she wondered why this happened, and would it ever happen again?

Chapter 2

Many days had passed since Abby's adventure at the carnival. Now and then the pretty black cat thought about the events of that day, and she would wonder if she would ever have another adventure like that. Before she gave it much thought, something would happen around the house and distract her. This morning, Abby had perched herself on the back of the couch and looked out the window. She had watched the Mr. and Mrs. leave for work, just like she did most days. Once their car was out of sight, Abby stayed there on the comfy couch, watching a brown sparrow. The little bird pecked at the seed in the bird feeder in the front yard. The kitty was motionless but for the twitch of her long tail. She watched the bird for a little while, then got bored with it. Abby stood up and walked down to the end of the couch, down the armrest, then jumped to the floor. She wandered around the main floor of the house, and her mind took her to the bottomless box and her friend Tiger. She smiled every time she thought of the fun they had together.

The long-tailed cat found plenty to do when she wanted to, or she would take a nap, which she often did. Right now she felt restless, and the black cat realized that she hadn't been back to the attic to check on it after licking her foot clean of the cotton candy. She felt an urge to return to the top room of the house. The yearning to go to the attic was very strong. Suddenly, she remembered that on the day of the first adventure, she had felt anxious, just like she felt now. Maybe her adventures weren't over yet! She got a little excited and was ready to find out. After a big stretch, the slick black cat ran up the stairs and headed for the spare bedroom.

Abby didn't stop running until she came to the tall mirror that hid the entrance to the attic stairs. She stopped for a moment when she saw her reflection in the mirror. She realized that she had grown into a very beautiful cat. She didn't look like a big kitten anymore. She noticed that she had a sleek, shiny black coat with a white bib and a very long black tail. She thought about when the Mrs. would brush her and tell her how pretty her fur was. Every day the Mr. would say how beautiful she was. Abby continued to look into the mirror and smiled inside as she thought of these things. Suddenly, her focus came back to why she was at the mirror, and she pressed the reflection of her foot with her front paw to release the magnetic latch that held the door closed. She heard the familiar metallic click, and then the mirrored gateway was open. The long-tailed cat crossed the entryway and looked up the stairs to the attic. As before, the sunshine was pouring into the attic through the window at the top of the stairs to brighten her path.

Abby's tummy began to twitch with anticipation, and it was then that Abby remembered she had a dream the night before about an adventure. Realizing this was what had happened the first time, she ran up the wooden stairs, taking two at a time, until she reached the large shadowy area. With a quick glance, Abby didn't see anything new or different in the room as she compared the current contents with those in her memory. It felt like it had been a long time since she was first up here. She could look another time for anything different. Right now, she only wanted to find the box. Would it send her on her way to another adventure? She wasted no time as she went to the far end of the attic. Through the rays of sunlight, she saw the cardboard box right where it had been the first time she saw it.

Abby quickly padded across the attic floor to get to the box. The cardboard flaps were folded over the opening, just like before. She reached over the top flap and pulled it toward her, then folded open the other three sections of the cardboard until the box was showing the entire opening. Abby wondered if she could see the entrance to the traveling portal. Looking into the box, the pretty cat could not see anything but darkness. Abby tingled all over and was full of energy. She was so excited her mouth was dry. She said aloud, "What am I waiting for?" and jumped into the cardboard square.

Although Abby had hoped there would not be a bottom to the box, she was still surprised to feel the floating sensation. Before she had time to ponder the drop, she landed softly on all four feet. Cats almost always land on their feet. There was a puff of powder and sparkly stars as Abby landed. She gathered her wits and popped her head out over the edge of the box. Her eyes grew in wonder as she took in the vision in front of her.

With no reluctance, the black cat jumped from the box and landed in cushy grass beside a large shade tree. She saw a luxurious park with rolling hills, lush green trees, and white benches sitting here and there. When she looked behind her, she saw a picturesque lake with a light mist rising toward the sky. There was no wind, and the view showed the lake surrounded by a mixture of hardwood and pine trees. The reflection of the plush trees and sky was a mirror image in the still water. The sky was blue and the air was warm. Abby looked toward the park and noticed beautiful flowers growing in several gardens. The traveling cat gazed up at the tree beside her,

paying attention to where her transportation box would be when it came time to head for home. Miss Longtail took a deep breath and started walking toward the lake, and the cushioned ground felt amazing under her paws. It was as soft as the carpet in the house, but cooler, and it felt wonderful between her toes. She started going down a small hill and noticed a multicolored cat sitting on the shoreline. It was white, black, and brown, and very pretty. Abby picked up her pace and padded down the hill to where the cat of many colors was sitting. The soft ground silenced Abby's steps, and the tricolored kitty didn't hear Abby's approach.

When the black cat was within earshot, she slowed and softly said, "Hello."

The cat turned to face the sound and asked, "Is your name Abby?"

Abby nodded, asking, "Who are you?"

"My name is Toochee. I had a dream that I had to come here today and I would make a new friend, a black cat with a long tail, and her name would be Abby."

Abby walked up to Toochee and sat down next to her. "I had a dream, too, that I would go on an adventure. My dream came true, and here I am! Where did you come from?" asked Abby.

Toochee pointed toward the water and said, "My family lives on the other side of the lake, just beyond those trees. You can't see the house, but it isn't very far." Abby was looking toward where the cat was pointing, and Toochee said, "There is a spa just up that hill behind us. I went up and looked around before you got here, and saw a bunch of places where we can be pampered. We are in for a treat today!"

Soft bells rang in the distance and interrupted Toochee's telling of their whereabouts. Abby looked at her new friend, and Toochee said, "Ah, the bells ringing means it is time for some tenderness. Follow me." With that, Toochee started running up the hill, away from the lake. Abby followed with great anticipation.

As they neared the top of the hill, Abby saw several small one-story buildings with a lot of the parklike grounds between them. Abby followed Toochee, who seemed to know right where to go. The new friend led them to a white-brick patio. There, the cats found two bowls each of fresh cat food, water, and cream. Toochee told Abby the food and drinks were there for them. Abby just had a sip of water, and Toochee said she might get something later. After the long-tailed cat had her refreshment, she scanned the area and was amazed at what she saw. On the patio were several tables set up in random fashion. Everything was white—the tables, chairs, and the buildings on the grounds. It was very pretty, with the contrast of the rich green grass. Near each building was a white sign with decorative green letters that indicated the service offered at that location. Abby noticed a few people walking about, strolling on the patio and along the white-brick sidewalks that connected all the buildings. The people were dressed in long white robes that flowed gracefully as they moved.

The two cats ventured off the patio onto the grass and sat down. Abby turned to her new friend and asked, "Toochee, was last night your first dream to come here?"

Toochee lay down, looked at Abby, and nodded. She said, "I remember dreaming about coming here, meeting a cat named Abby, and spending the day getting pampered with the new friend. When I woke up, I had a strong urge to come here."

Abby thought about Tiger having the dream to meet her at the carnival and wondered if they were connected somehow. Abby was about to tell the multicolored cat about her previous adventure when Toochee said, "I have heard my lady tell my man about this spa, so I knew what to expect, but I've never done anything like this before. What about you?"

Abby grinned, saying, "My situation is a little different, and you may find it hard to believe. I still can't believe it!"

Toochee looked at the soft-haired cat with interest and said, "Do tell."

Abby lay down, crossed one front paw over the other, and began to share her story. She told of her family's move, having the dream, and the desire to explore the attic where she found the box. She told Toochee of the trip to the carnival, meeting Tiger, and the safe return home. As Toochee listened in amazement, Abby shared her interest in the box again that morning, how she ventured to the attic, and her leap of faith, which brought her here today. Toochee was stunned and asked, "Do you ever wonder how or why this happens?"

Abby nodded. "I do, but mostly, I just enjoy it."

Both cats giggled.

Abby Longtail looked at her new friend and said, "Let's talk about today. What kinds of things will we do? Are they going to pet us all day?"

Graceful Toochee purred in delightful anticipation and said, "Oh, they will do more than pet us. There are several different spa stations that we can try. Each building name shows what pampering is offered. I saw Massage Manor. I bet we could each get a rubdown there!"

Abby's eyes widened, and she said, "That sounds good. What else can we do?"

Toochee continued telling her new friend about the other things the spa offered. "We can get our teeth whitened, take a mud bath or a milk bath, have facials, have our

hair colored, sit in a sauna, and even get our paws scrubbed and claws clipped. There may not be enough time to try everything."

Abby had a puzzled look on her face, and Toochee asked her what she was thinking about. Abby said, "Milk bath? That is just silly! Milk is for drinking"

Both cats laughed.

"We should probably get going," Abby said. "Toochee, you pick where we go first. I will try anything except the hair coloring. I don't think my Mrs. would like it if I came home as a blonde."

Toochee stood up and said, "If we are going to have all kinds of body treatments, I think we should get dirty first. Do you want to melt into the mud bath before we do anything else?"

Abby nodded, then lifted her white-tipped front paw and pointed to a building off to the left of the patio. "There is the Mud Bath Bungalow." The cats were giggling, and both were wondering about what the mud would feel like.

"Sounds gooey," said Toochee. "I am not sure it is normal for cats to get into mud," she said.

Abby stopped and looked back at her new friend, and laughed. "Perfect, because there is nothing normal about these adventures!"

Toochee said, "The Mrs. has said the mud bath is her favorite thing here because it is so warm and cozy, and she always comes home clean as a whistle."

Smiling, the black cat replied, "That sounds pretty good!"

The cats arrived at the entrance of the building. "I'm ready!" said Toochee, and Abby said, "Me too." The cats were anxious to experience the mud bath and see what it was all about.

The etched glass double doors separated automatically as the cats neared the entrance. The duo went through the opening and stopped as they took in all the beauty. There were statues and pretty flowers. It was a very relaxing setting. Across from the entrance, two large mirrors soared from the floor to the ceiling. Toochee pointed at the mirrors and said, "I think we have to go there. I remember hearing my Mrs. tell my Mr. that the mirrors will open up to the mud bath."

The cats padded through the lobby area. When they got to the mirrors, the reflecting glass opened inwardly, so the cats passed through and found themselves in the mud bath area. The room was lit by many candles of all shapes and sizes placed here and there, and the soft glow gave an instant sense of relaxation. Just ahead of the cats was a floor made of square ceramic tiles. In the middle of the room was a large shallow pool of mud. Against one of the walls were several dressing rooms where humans could change their clothes. The two cats looked at each other. Without a word, they headed for the gooey pool. The friends stepped onto the tiles that surrounded the pool, and they felt the coolness of the tiles on the pads of their paws. They took a moment and looked around the room. On each corner of the mud bath was a stack of thick white terrycloth towels. Although the walls were dark, a skylight let in sunshine, softened by the smoky gray glass of the window. A grated walking path led to a door marked SHOWERS. Abby pointed to it and said, "I guess we won't have to go too far to get cleaned up."

Abby and Toochee were quiet as they gazed down at the mud and then looked at each other. They were both wondering what the warm mud would feel like. It was such a calm place that neither kitty wanted to make any noise, but Toochee looked up and grinned, saying, "Last one in is a rotten egg!" and stepped into the pool that had the appearance of chocolate pudding. Not wanting to be left behind, Abby quickly followed, and the two cats were soon covered with goo from their head to their toes, and they were surprised that the warmth and the thickness of the mud felt so wonderful.

They melted down in the warmness, and there were "Ooohs" and "Ahhhhs" coming from the new friends, with lots and lots of purring. Abby was the first to speak up, and she only had one thing to say: "Pppuuurrrfffeeeccccttt!" Toochee was on her back with just her head and four paws sticking out of the mud. Abby was relaxing, too, with only her head and the tip of her long tail exposed.

The cats lounged, rolled, and relaxed in the warm, wet earth, and they were having a wonderful time. The room was quiet as they soaked in the sensation of the mud. After a bit, they heard a distant ding, then another, and another. Softly, Abby said, "The chimes must mean it is time to get out. If we are going to try any more of the spa experience, we better get moving." Slowly the two climbed out of the muddy pool. Each cat wiped down as much of the goo as they could before they went to get rinsed off. They padded along the grate to the shower room.

Toochee said, "I usually don't like getting wet, but I think this will be different."

The shower room looked similar to the rest of the spa. White tiles on the floor and walls, white towels on white counters. The room was welcoming, with soft lights, so it wasn't too bright. There were individual stalls with several showerheads in each one, allowing the water to come from all directions and from many levels. The cats could pick the water pressure they wanted from the different heads. Abby said, "I am just going to get in and get out," and she headed for the shower directly in front of her. Toochee entered the shower right next to her friend. Both of the cats were covered with mud, and they looked silly. Once Abby was in the stall, the water came on in a mist, followed by a pleasant spray to wash the mud away. Each cat applied sweet-smelling shampoo to their fur to help remove the dirt, and it was coming off quite easily. *Nothing could go wrong here,* thought Abby.

Once clean, the two felines came out of the shower room. They were both saying how good the morning had been while they dried off with the thick white towels. The cats tossed the damp towels into a basket marked WET TOWELS and headed to a large set of stainless steel double doors. As the cats approached the way out, the two doors opened automatically, sliding apart and disappearing into the surrounding wall. They stepped through and entered a long hallway. They moved along rather quickly as they saw another set of double doors at the far end of the hall, topped with a red EXIT sign. The passage walls were made of mirrors, and each cat's reflection rebounded from one side of the hall to the other. The space looked very large and appeared to be full of hundreds of cats, all duplicates of the original pair. Toochee grinned, saying, "This is weird," and took off running to the far end of the hall, and Abby followed suit. They reached the doors about the same time, and just as before, the doors slid apart and opened up to the beautiful patio they had seen before.

The two cats walked over to where the cat-size bowls were sitting, and each had a quick bite and a drink of cream. As they finished up their snack, Abby said, "Before we do anything else, I would just like to thank you for being a part of this adventure with me. We may not get to see all the sights or try all the treatments, but I have had a lot of fun here." Toochee responded with an applause of paws, and Abby continued. "We should figure out what we want to do next."

"Okay!" said Toochee, and she headed for one of the white-brick pathways.

Abby looked at her new friend and thought to herself, *How lucky we are to be part of these magical adventures!* and hurried to catch up.

Toochee asked, "What spa treatment would you like to do now since it is your turn to pick?"

Abby knew exactly what she wanted to do and replied, "Earlier today we talked about how nice a massage would be, so I would like to do that."

Toochee didn't hesitate at all and stated that she would love to try a massage. Abby reacted with a smile and added that someday she would like to try a yoga class. "Maybe we could all learn some new stretching techniques. I love to stretch!"

Toochee was looking at her paw and changed the subject by asking, "After the rubdown, can we get our nails done?" Toochee picked up her paw and stretched it out so she could look at each of her long curved nails. "I don't know about you, but my nails need clipping!"

Abby copied Toochee's actions by extending her claws and decided they needed some attention too. Then Abby said, "Clipping or not, it will feel good to have someone pay attention to my paws."

Toochee asked, "Then we agree that we will get a massage and then a manicure… or a pedicure. Which is it, a manicure or a pedicure? They will be working on our paws. Should we call it a pawdicure?"

The cats laughed, and Abby answered, "It doesn't matter as long as they do it. The plan sounds wonderful!"

The two cats high-fived their front paws together in agreement and headed for the building marked MASSAGE MANOR.

They walked along on the same sidewalk that led to the mud bath then turned onto a path that branched off to another building, the building where they were going to get their rubdowns. The trails were intertwined, making it trouble-free to go between buildings by staying on the walkways and following the signs. The channels were lovely, so white, with pretty flowers adorning the paths. Massage Manor was a little farther away from the patio, and the cats picked up their pace to get there more quickly.

As they arrived at the glass double doors, the sensor reacted to the presence of the spa guests and opened. The cats entered the building and walked into a lobby area. They saw many rooms on both sides of the entrance hall. As they walked along, they noticed that each room's entrance had a curtain that was pulled back and held in place by fresh flowers. All the rooms looked the same. Each had a privacy area near the back wall partially hidden by a decorative folding screen, with the massage table set up in the center of the room. Smaller white tables and cabinets held lotions, towels, and other supplies that were needed by the staff to do their work. Nothing was cluttered or out of place.

A soft voice spoke through an overhead speaker and said, "Welcome. Guests only need to enter the room of his or her choice, and the therapy will begin."

The cats huddled together for a bit, not sure if they really understood what was about to happen. Abby whispered, "I have a feeling that once we pick the room, it won't be long and we will be getting the rubdown of our lives."

Toochee agreed and started walking to the door closest to her. She looked back at the pretty, long-tailed cat. "This is exciting! See you when the massage is done…if I haven't melted onto the floor! Ha ha!"

Abby smiled and followed Toochee's lead by picking the room next to the one her friend had chosen. As they walked past the curtains, they looked at each other and Toochee said, "Enjoy!"

Once the cats were in the massage rooms, the flowers that held the curtains magically released and fell onto the floor. The breeze of the curtains closing enhanced the fragrance of the flowers and filled each room with a gentle scent that stayed the entire time. As Abby Longtail gracefully jumped up on the massage table, a part of the back wall started to slide away—there was a hidden entrance that had blended in with the decorations. A beautiful lady wearing a white gown emerged. She smiled and, speaking very softly, said, "Hello. I am your therapist and will be giving your massage today. Before we start, do you need anything?" Abby shook her head no, and the therapist pushed a small button on the wall. Soft music began to play, and the woman motioned for Abby to lie down on her tummy. Selecting a soft white sheet from one of the cabinets, the therapist opened the sheet and gently draped it on the cat's back. Next, she pressed one of the lotion's pumps with one hand and caught the dispensed massage oil in her other hand. She rubbed her hands together, then began at Abby's neck. With the most amazing touch, she began to knead the cat's muscles. The woman commented quietly, "Your fur is so soft and beautiful." The therapist's fingertips worked their way around the cat's ears, under her chin, everywhere Abby loved to be pampered, and she purred loudly in appreciation.

This is wonderful, Abby thought, and with a deep sigh, she became completely relaxed.

Time passed quickly as the massage continued down Abby's back, each leg and each paw, even her long tail. Every muscle was pampered, and it provided a wonderful feeling of relaxation. The therapist had been quiet since she told Abby how pretty her fur was, focusing on the task at hand. She finished the massage by a final touch, gently rubbing around Abby's neck. Speaking softly, the woman told Abby that her time was up and she hoped that the experience had been enjoyable. Abby purred as she rose to her feet, then stretched as cats do. The long-tailed cat showed her appreciation by rubbing her head and shoulder against the therapist. The woman gave the black cat an affectionate pat on the head, then picked up her client and gently set her on the floor. The pampering lady pulled the curtain open for Abby to exit, then turned around and disappeared through the hidden entry with her white gown flowing behind her.

Abby walked slowly into the lobby, looking for her friend. She saw Toochee coming from her massage room with a peaceful expression on her face. They approached each other, and Toochee was the first to speak. She cooed as she said, "Oh, Abby, that was great! Massages were definitely the right choice. It would be nice to come here every day," and she purred as she arched her back into a cat stretch.

Abby whispered, "I agree. That felt wonderful!"

Walking side by side, the two cats headed for the sliding glass doors. When the doors were open, the friends passed through the opening and went into the yard. Abby noticed that the sun was in the western sky. She knew their day was drawing to a close. The cats continued to walk down the sidewalk in the direction of the patio, and Abby asked Toochee, "Do you think we have enough time to get our nails trimmed?"

Toochee nodded and said, "Let's walk this way," pointing her paw ahead of them. "I see a sign that says TENDER TRIMMING. It looks like the place we need to go to get our nails done and it shouldn't take very long." Abby's eyes followed the direction of her friend's paw, and together the duo walked to the sign. They continued on to the white building that provided the nail service. This building was smaller than any of the others they had been in, but it looked very similar. The cats went through the sliding glass doors and stepped onto a cool marble floor. There was soft music playing, and Abby piped up. "I only want my nails to be clipped. Toochee, are you thinking of doing any other paw pampering?"

Toochee replied, "I would like to have some buffing to keep my nails from snagging on anything."

Abby said, "I hadn't thought of that. It sounds like a great idea."

"Okay," said Toochee, "let's do it." Then she added, "You know, Abby, I have never been crazy about getting my nails clipped, but I am looking forward to this!"

Abby said, "I know what you mean. I usually don't like it when my nails get cut at home. I have a feeling that this is going to be different."

Across the room, they saw a sign that read PURR-FECT PAMPERING, and there were cat paw prints all around the lettering for decoration. Below the sign they saw a stainless steel platform, about one cat-step higher than the regular floor. As the two friends headed toward the raised area, a gentle voice was heard from a speaker on the wall. "Please step onto the platform in front of you and place your paws into the impressions."

Abby and Toochee stood at the edge of the silver-colored stage. They could see that the steel was set up to pamper four cats at one time. Each cat station was set up for clipping or buffing and also offered the option for acrylic sleeves for the nails. The sleeves would keep the cats from needing to scratch as well as keeping the nails looking their best. Looking down at the platform in front of them, they each saw a section of the stainless steel with four paw prints embedded into the metal. The girls looked at each other. Toochee shrugged her shoulders and stepped up and placed all four paws into the molded areas. Abby was a bit reluctant, but she watched as Toochee did as directed, and nothing bad happened. More relaxed, the black cat mimicked her friend's action. She stepped up and placed her feet in the impressions on the platform in the neighboring workstation. The speaker crackled slightly, and the voice spoke again. "Please spread your toes out to reveal your nails and hold them in that position. A laser will be used to trim your nails. It is quick, painless, and will be done to all your toes at the same time." Abby winked at Toochee, took a deep breath, and spread her toes. In an instant, there was a muffled zapping sound, and then a red light ran under the platform. Just as quickly, the noise and the light were gone. The soft speaker voice returned. "The laser trimming is complete. If you prefer buffing, please remain in place. Acrylic sleeves can be added after the buffing, if you choose."

Neither cat moved, and Abby waved her long tail in a sense of excitement and heard Toochee whisper, "This is pretty cool!"

The voice in the speaker continued. "Again, please spread your toes to reveal your nails, and the buffing will begin. This process will take just a few moments and, like the clipping, will happen to all the nails at once. It will be gentle and relaxing. Thank you."

With that, the cats again spread their toes in the metal paw prints. An electronic buffer with a very soft humming sound was sensed under the platform, and soft strokes to the nails were felt by the cats. It was very soothing, and within just a few seconds, everything stopped. The voice spoke again, informing the customers, "If you would like the acrylic sleeves to be added to your nails, please remain on the platform. If not, please step down. We hope you have enjoyed your experience at Tender Trimming!"

Abby and Toochee stepped down and headed toward the center of the lobby. Then the cats sat down and both started talking at once about how much they loved the way their nails were cared for. They were smiling and talking to each other in a jumble and expressing the same thing, that the experience was great! Abby said, "Toochee, may I see your paws?" Her friend held up a front paw and spread her toes wide for the black cat. The nails were all clipped evenly and were buffed shiny and smooth. There were no jagged edges or rough ends. "Wow, they look great!" said Abby. Toochee then asked to see Abby's and nodded with approval when Abby showed her the manicured claws. Toochee said, "Getting our nails done here was worth it!" Abby nodded. The friends trotted to the doors, and just before leaving, Abby turned around and shouted, "Thank you!" and then the freshly manicured cats were outside.

The duo followed the sidewalk as it wound around and led them back to the beautiful white patio. Abby said, "This was such a special day. I am glad we came here for our adventure."

Toochee replied, "I agree. I feel so good from that massage. Now with my nails done, I am thinking about a nice nap. I wish I could curl up and take a snooze before I start my journey home. Are you tired?"

Abby realized she was a little sleepy and said so. "I won't take a nap, though, until I am back home. I have to go to the magical box to get me there."

Toochee softly said, "You are lucky to travel in that box, and I know that it is time for you to get ready to leave."

Abby and Toochee's eyes met, and they both knew their time together was almost over.

The two cats started walking toward the lake and to the magical box. "We better hurry," said Toochee. "I have to get home before dinner." The two cats picked up their pace, and they ran over the rolling hills and arrived at their destination rather quickly.

The cats rubbed shoulders, their tails entwined, and they each gave the other their best wishes. Abby looked at Toochee and then hung her head. With teary eyes, she said, "I will miss you, my friend, and I hope to see you again."

Toochee nudged her friend and whispered in her ear, "I will miss you, too, and hope someday we can meet again. I hate to leave, but I better get going," and the two cats walked together to the edge of the cardboard carrier. "I'll wait until I know you are on your way," said Toochee.

Abby patted her friend's shoulder, smiled, and said, "Until next time!" then leaped into the bottomless box.

Falling freely, but not too fast, the sleek black cat traveled through the mysterious space. The next thing she knew, she was waking up in the spare room of her family's home, curled up on the guest bed. Abby felt as if it must be late in the day, after all she had been through, and she thought she should get downstairs before the Mr. and Mrs. got home. She jumped from the bed. Landing softly on the carpeted floor, she quickly padded out the bedroom door and down the hall to the stairway that led to the living room. Everything was quiet, and Abby scurried down the stairs and jumped up

on the couch. She looked out the big window to watch for her Mr. and Mrs. to pull in the driveway. She got anxious as she looked outside. The sky seemed to be darkening just slightly, much like it did most days before suppertime. Abby thought about what she had done that day. Had she really gone to a spa and made a new friend, or had it been a dream? She remembered the manicure and looked at her front paws. She lifted one leg and projected her nails, and giggled as she saw they were perfectly trimmed and buffed to a lustrous shine. She knew that she was a lucky cat to have gone to the carnival and met Tiger, and then to the spa where she met Toochee.

Abby went out to the kitchen and had a drink of water. She returned to the couch and watched a few birds come to the feeder. She was so relaxed she took a little catnap.

The black cat woke up rested. She sat up and thought about her day. Abby thought she should make sure the mirrored door was closed, and started up the stairs when she heard the door open to the kitchen and knew the Mr. and Mrs. were home. The black cat scurried down to greet her family and let them know they were missed. Abby ran to the kitchen and wrapped herself around the Mr.'s legs and meowed softly. The man bent down and picked up his little girl, stroking her head as she purred in delight. The Mr. spoke softly to Abby, telling her what a good kitty she was. The Mrs. came near and scratched Abby under her chin, then she asked the long-tailed cat if she was hungry. Abby perked up and wiggled until the Mr. set her down on the floor. The cat went over to the Mrs., who set a bowl of tasty morsels down in front of her, and Abby began to eat. The Mrs. told the Mr. that she was going to make their supper, and the Mr. replied that he would be in his recliner, going through the day's mail.

Abby ate all her meal and licked the bowl clean. She went to the Mrs. and nudged the woman's ankle. The Mrs. squatted down to pet the black cat, starting at her head and running her hand all along her back to the tip of her long tail. "My goodness, you have such soft fur, and it seems extra soft today." Abby thought of the oils and lotions used with her massage and purred. "Okay, kitty, scoot from the kitchen so I can cook." Abby complied and headed for the living room to seek out the Mr.'s lap. The graceful black cat made a gentle leap onto the arm of the recliner, where the man was resting in his chair, reading his newspaper. She tiptoed her way over his arm, one foot at a time, until she was standing on his lap. The man knew his fur baby wanted his undivided attention, and he put his paper down on an end table. The man chuckled as he caressed the cat's back, then said, "Abby, last week I promised the Mrs. that I would cut your nails. I guess we should do that before dinner." The Mr. reached into his pants pocket and pulled out a special nail clipper just for cats. He turned Abby in his lap so he could hold her paw and extend her nails. Much to his surprise, her nails were perfectly cut and smooth. Abby was grinning to herself as she thought of the laser at the spa, and he whispered, "Well, I guess the Mrs. beat me to it." Abby curled up in the Mr.'s lap and it wasn't long before both the kitty and the man were sound asleep.

The Mr. and Abby both stirred when the Mrs. called out that dinner was ready. The man picked Abby off his lap and set her on the floor, then rose and headed for the kitchen. The long-tailed cat started to follow the man, then stopped. She remembered she needed to check on the attic door, so she changed direction and padded up the stairway. When she got to the spare room, she saw the attic door was ajar. Curiosity got the best of her, and she wondered, if she jumped in the box again, if she would go on another adventure. She headed for the attic to see if there was another trip for her waiting in the bottomless box. She sat next to the box, her long silky tail twitching back and forth as she contemplated the jump. The only way she would know if or where she might go would be to make the leap, so in she jumped.

The landing was quick and hard as Abby's feet fell on the bottom of the cardboard box. The bottomless box wasn't bottomless after all. Abby walked around in a circle inside the four walls of the container. She wondered what had happened to the portal. Slowly Abby stepped out of the carton and began to walk toward the stairs. When she stepped down on the first step, she looked back toward the box in confusion. Abby lumbered down the attic stairs and pushed the mirrored door closed with her head, making sure the magnet caught to keep it sealed. What did this mean? Were her adventures over?

Chapter 3

Every once in a while, Abby would venture to the attic to see if another adventure was available to her. She would jump in the cardboard box and go nowhere. One time she moved the box to another spot on the attic floor and hopped in, but that hadn't made a difference. She wondered why it had worked before but not now. She knew she was lucky to have had the time with Tiger and Toochee, and she was very content to be home with her family. Time passed, and Abby hardly thought about the box anymore.

One wintery day, the Mrs. told Abby that she and the Mr. weren't going to work but instead were going to do some shopping for Christmas. Abby knew the holiday was not far off, as the Mrs. had been decorating the inside of the house with a pine tree, pine boughs, and all kinds of snowmen and jingle bells. The Mr. had been just as busy outside, putting up lights on the house and the trees in the yard, and setting up the manger that told the Christmas Story. All the decorations had been stored up in the attic since they moved to this house. The Mr. and Mrs. snuggled their cat for a bit before leaving, and as she always did, the black cat ran to the couch to watch them leave the driveway. Once they were out of sight, Abby had a familiar tingling in her tummy, and she knew she had to visit the attic. Over the last few weeks, Abby had wondered if the family had done anything with the cardboard box when they were bringing the Christmas decoration totes down from the attic. With the house to herself, she wasted no time getting to the top level of the house, where her previous adventures had begun. The pretty cat breathed a sigh of relief when she saw the box was still there, sitting in the same spot it had always been. Abby padded over to the box, pulled back the flaps, and looked inside. She felt excitement stir and, with a leap of faith, jumped into the box.

The gentle fall felt more like floating, and before Abby could give it much thought, she landed softly and with the familiar puff and twinkling of stars. Without hesitation, she popped her head up over the edge of the box. She saw trees, trees, and more trees, of all different kinds and sizes. Fall leaves of red, yellow, and crispy brown, as well as pine needles, and twigs covered the ground. Nearby, there was a gravel walking path that looked like the driveway at her house, and she could see some really large rocks near the path. Slowly she crept from the box and looked around. She wondered if she would meet a new friend like she had before. Abby

headed toward the large rocks. As she got closer, she thought she saw the tip of a cat's tail on the other side of the biggest rock. She jumped up to the top of the large piece of stone and stopped short when she saw a huge cat with black-and-white fur.

   Quickly the big cat turned around and grinned when seeing Abby. With a friendly smile, the cat spoke in a deep voice. "There you are, if you are Abby!" Abby Longtail nodded. "My name is Oreo, and I live nearby. I had a dream last night that made me think that if I came here today, I would meet a black cat named Abby and she would have a very long tail."

At that moment, Abby recalled that she had a dream the night before, too, and that was what enticed her to go to the attic. The adventuresome cat smiled as she hopped down from the big rock and stood near Oreo. "My names is Abby, Abby Longtail," and she stroked her long tail for emphasis. "What else happened in your dream?" Abby asked.

Oreo replied, "We go on a nature hike through the woods and the trail takes us to a big lake."

Abby said, "That sounds great! Have you ever gone on a nature hike before?"

Oreo nodded and said, "Yes, I have been on some great walks with the girl at my house. She likes this path, but I have never been here. I have heard her tell her friends about it." The black-and-white cat went on. "I was exploring a little before you arrived. Up ahead is a sign with pictures of where we are and what we might see on the trail, including some waterfalls. I saw a water fountain, too, and could use a drink before we start on the trail."

Abby said, "A sip of water sounds good."

The trailhead of the footpath was just past the water fountain, where each feline sipped eagerly at the refreshing beverage. Now ready, the two new friends were on their way. Abby thought the trail looked as wide as the driveway at her house, and as they padded along, she noticed that just a bit ahead of them, the walkway curved out of sight. They walked along and had general conversation about the path, the pretty colored leaves, and the wild mushrooms growing here and there. After a bit, neither cat was talking as they meandered along.

Abby broke the silence by asking, "Well, new friend, tell me about you."

Oreo answered, "That might be a long story!"

That piqued Abby's interest, and she prodded the black-and-white cat to continue by saying, "I want to hear about your family, but first, I have to know. Are you named after an Oreo cookie, because your fur is black-and-white?"

Oreo chuckled and replied, "Yes, black-and-white and *yummy*!" The two cats giggled together, and Oreo said, "At least that is what the lady of the house says!" The two cats giggled a little more, and then Oreo told his story.

"I was living at an animal shelter," he said, "when a woman and a young girl came in looking to adopt a cat."

Abby was confused and interrupted her new friend. "What is an animal shelter?"

Oreo said, "A shelter is a place where animals can live if they don't have a safe place to stay. I don't know about other shelters, but there were cats and dogs at the

shelter where I was. It was like a little home with different rooms for us. The folks who worked there took very good care of us and made sure we were healthy and happy. Then people who are looking to get a pet can come to the shelter and find one they connect with, and they all go home together to live happily ever after."

"Wow," said Abby, "I didn't know that there were places like that. It is nice that there is a place for animals to go to."

"Yes," said Oreo. "I heard some stories from some of the stray cats who were living outside on the streets all of the time—hungry, wet, cold. They were very thankful to be at the shelter, where they were loved by the volunteers and the people that work there. In time they went home with good families."

Abby felt tugs at her heart as she heard about the animals in the shelter. She stopped walking, and her emotions were choking her up. Even though she didn't know her new friend very well, she asked, "Oreo, how did you come to be there?"

Oreo realized Abby wasn't next to him on the path, and he stopped and looked back. He saw Abby's face and immediately put her at ease when he said, "Oh, Abby, don't fret. It doesn't matter how I got there. What matters is that I did get there *and* they took care of me until my family took me home. Walk with me and I will tell you more."

The sleek black cat walked up to be side by side to her companion, and Oreo continued.

"I really don't remember being anywhere but the shelter. I was very young and was there with my two sisters and brother, plus some other kittens that became our friends. Because I was so young, I don't remember a whole lot. All the kittens were together in a room with cubby holes to hide in, scratch posts to stretch on, and towers to climb. The shelter workers and volunteers came in several times a day and would play with us, brush us, and snuggle with all of us. They taught us that we could trust them and we shouldn't bite when being held or groomed. It was nice. Sometimes strangers would visit, and they usually would take one of the cats or kittens home with them. I saw that happen a few times during my stay. Then one day, a lady and her young daughter were visiting the shelter and they came into the kitten room. The girl picked me up and started petting me very gently. It wasn't very long before she looked at her mom and said, 'I love this kitten, Mom. He looks like an Oreo cookie, and I think he is yummy!' That was the day I went to my forever home with the girl and her mom. Every day since, the lady tells me that I am yummy when she pets me."

Abby giggled as she asked, "That doesn't mean she will eat you, does it?"

Oreo looked surprised, then laughed. "No, you silly cat. She just likes to tell me that I am sweet, but she uses *yummy* for the word! I try to be a good cat, because I want to stay with them forever. The shelter was a good place to stay, but I love my home. What about you, Abby? Where did you come from?"

The two continued to walk along as Abby said, "Mine is simple. I don't remember ever being anywhere other than with the Mr. and Mrs. There aren't any little people there, and a while ago, we moved to a new house. The new house is where I found the bottomless box, which is what brought me here. You didn't see it, but I arrived here in a cardboard box."

As the cats meandered down the trail, Abby told Oreo about her family, her dreams, and her adventures since they moved to the new house. The black-and-white cat said, "Wow. That is incredible! You are really lucky!"

Abby said, "I think so too. I like making new friends and going on these adventures. When I get home, it seems like a dream, but I always seem to find a clue that lets me know the adventure was real."

Oreo asked, "Can you go on an adventure anytime you want?"

Abby shook her head and said, "No. I wondered that myself, and a few times I went up to the box and jumped in just to see what would happen, and I didn't go anywhere. I realized that if I ever got to go on another adventure, that would be fine, but I love my family and being with them." Then Abby added, "I always have a dream that makes me want to go jump into the cardboard box. It must be something like the dream that brought you here today."

Oreo nodded in understanding and replied, "The dreams seem to play a big part in these exciting journeys."

The two friends followed the path as it went around a sharp bend. Oreo looked to one side and saw a shallow river. The trail began to narrow as it followed the river's course. Oreo pointed out the river to Abby, and they walked over to get a good look. They watched the dark water break over rocks as it flowed. The cats were quiet as they went along, watching the current of the water.

Suddenly, Oreo stopped and said, "Hey, do you hear that?" Abby came to a halt and listened. There was a noise off in the distance that sounded like a strong wind.

"What is that?" asked Abby, but Oreo didn't hear her. He had started to run on the path in the direction of the noise.

Abby picked up her pace and Oreo glanced over his shoulder and shouted, "Come on!" Abby ran as fast as she could to catch up. Oreo was obviously excited as he ran, and then he exclaimed, "It's a waterfall!" The two cats ran faster, and the roar of the water grew louder and louder. When the waterfall came into view, the friends stopped to take in the beautiful sight. There were "Ooohs," "Aaahs," and lots of "Wows!" It wasn't a big waterfall, but it was very powerful. From the top to the bottom, there were six gradual tiers that the water tumbled over. It was wider at the top, narrowing at the bottom, where the falls ended and the water bubbled into the shallow river the cats had seen earlier.

Man-made fence along the water's edge protected the onlookers from falling into the river. Oreo said that he wanted to touch the moving water. He approached the edge, and Abby shouted for him to be careful. The drop from the bank to the water was much too far for the kitty to be able to reach his goal. That didn't stop Oreo from trying. He crouched down, stretched under the fence, and leaned over the bank, reaching down as far as he could, but was not close enough to get his paw wet. Abby chuckled, saying, "Come on, you silly cat! Maybe you can touch some water farther up the river. If you keep doing that, you might fall in and get all wet!"

The cats backtracked the few steps to return to the path. The trail had an uphill grade, and when they reached the crest of the hill, they were at the top of the waterfall. They stopped for a few minutes, amazed by the beauty and the strong force of the water. Where the falls met the river at the bottom of the falls, bubbles and white foam swirled. Just a short distance from the base of the falls, the water was dark from the minerals in the ground. Even so, it was extremely clear, and the cats could see the sandy bottom and every rock and branch in the stream. Oreo was studying the water, almost in a trance, and Abby asked, "What are you looking for?"

Oreo didn't take his eyes off the water, saying, "I was just wondering if I might see a fish. I thought I would try to touch the water here, too, but the current is too strong."

The cats started walking again. There were a few little turns just before the two friends came to a low walking bridge that went over the river. The bridge was made of wooden slats and had side railings that offered gaps the cats could look through and see the water. They stopped in the center of the bridge to take in the sight. Oreo looked through one of the openings and sighed. "No fish here either."

"Let's keep going," said Abby, and the two cats crossed the remainder of the bridge.

They hadn't gone very far when Oreo stated, "Wow! Look at the drop-off!" He pointed toward an area off to the side of where they were walking. The ground had cut away to a deep ravine. As Abby backed away from the bluff, she whined, "Meow! That gives me the heebie-jeebies!"

The path veered away from the river, and as the cats followed a turn, they came upon a wooden platform. It was a scenic overlook for the waterfall. The platform was surrounded on three sides by rails to protect the viewers from falling. As the cats walked closer to the wooden stage, they could hear the force of water like they had before. The kitties couldn't see the water from where they were. They went up the two steps to go on to the platform and then walked out to see the sight. Abby slowed down as they neared the far side of the platform, not wanting to get too close. Oreo boldly walked to the edge to get a good view. He noticed that Abby wasn't beside him, and he looked back.

"Come on, Abby," said Oreo. "Don't you want to see the waterfall?"

Abby hung her head and shook it back and forth, twitching her long tail. Oreo noticed that Abby was trembling and went to her. Still looking down, she whispered, "I am afraid that I might fall if I go too close to the edge."

Oreo wrapped a front leg around his new friend in support, saying, "Oh, Abby, I won't let you fall. How about if we go together? I won't leave your side."

Abby shook her head no, and Oreo continued to be supportive. "There is nothing wrong with being afraid of dangerous things, but this place was built to hold people, and a lot of them. You don't have to go to the edge. Do you think you could take a step or two and see if you can see the waterfall just by being up a little closer?"

Abby looked Oreo in the eyes, and asked, "Will you stay with me?"

Oreo gave her a little smile and replied, "Of course. Let's take a step and see what we can see."

The two cats walked together slowly until they were just a short distance from the guardrail. The view was incredible as they looked across the deep crevice and saw an amazing waterfall on the other side, surrounded by the splendor of Mother Nature in bright reds, yellows and greens. Abby and Oreo both gasped as they watched the water cascading down several steep ledges of rocks. It was a long way down, and the two kitties couldn't see the bottom from where they were standing.

Abby said, "Do you think we might see the bottom of the falls if we took another step toward the edge?"

Oreo replied, "I don't think so. There are too many trees in the ravine, so getting closer won't get us a better look. The falls just blend into the treetops."

"Wow," said Abby, "this is really beautiful!" She looked at Oreo, and whispered, "Thank you for understanding."

Oreo winked and leaned into his friend, rubbing shoulders like a buddy will do. "Look," said Abby, pointing toward the waterfall. "I think that this is the same waterfall that we looked at before the bridge—from the other side!"

Oreo agreed. "You're right. See the flat area there near the top?" The cookie cat pointed at the falls. "That is where I tried to reach down and touch the water. Who would have guessed the falls would be this big from a different viewpoint?"

The cats stayed on the platform for a few more minutes, pointing out highlights to each other. After a bit, Abby said, "We better get going. I want to see as much as we can today." Oreo agreed, and they backed off from the platform and returned to the path.

The trail veered away from the river and went deeper into the forest. The cats visited as they went along, occasionally noticing movements in nature. Abby chased a butterfly. Oreo went after a chipmunk until it ran down a hole. He tried to pin down a toad with his front paw, but every time he would get close, the toad would hop just out of his reach. Abby had fun watching Oreo try to get one step up on the toad until the cookie cat finally gave up and the friends moved on.

The cats came to a set of steps that were carved into the ground. The two took the stairs and followed the trail as it meandered through the forest. Rounding a large curve, the colorful woods opened up to a high blue sky and an enormous drop-off that overlooked an amazing body of water that appeared to go on forever. The sunlight glistened off the water like twinkling diamonds, and the high-banked shoreline was just as impressive from centuries of erosion.

"This is beautiful!" said Oreo. "Look at the water…it never ends."

"Is this an ocean?" asked Abby.

"No," replied Oreo, "but it is a great big lake! Isn't it fabulous?"

Abby nodded, and they sat down to look at the water and the beauty of nature. They were back far enough from the bluff that Abby wasn't concerned about falling.

Oreo said, "I think we might be able to see more of the shoreline if we keep going," and the friends started walking again.

The cats were quiet as they moved along, taking in the sights. Abby broke the silence and commented how far down it was from the cliff edge to the water below. The worn trail was just a stone's toss from the edge of the bluff. Oreo remembered how Abby felt about the edge of the platform, so he maneuvered around the black-tailed cat so that he was on the cliff side of the path to help Abby relax. There was plenty of room on the trail for the two cats to walk side by side, and Abby was grateful for the support from her friend. Oreo pointed out different items to help Abby keep her mind off the cliff's edge. A variety of withered wildflowers and berry bushes lined the path and were a good distraction. The trail turned slightly away from the shoreline, then emerged into an open area with a few spots set up for picnics or for hikers to pitch tents and camp.

Rays of sunlight peaked through the treetops and shone down on the cats, making them warm and cozy. Abby lay down on a soft patch of moss and asked, "Do you think I have time for a catnap? I sure could use one."

Oreo joined her on the natural green cushion and curled up beside her. "You read my mind, my friend," he said and rested his head on his paws before closing his eyes. Abby curled into a tight ball, wrapped her tail around her body, and soon they were both in a deep slumber.

A black raven calling out to his companions woke the sleeping felines. Both cats stirred and yawned before they stood up, arched their backs, and then stretched out long, as cats do.

"That was a nice nap," said Abby.

"I was out like a rock!" Oreo answered back. "I think we should start back before it gets dark. We want to make sure we both get home in the daylight."

The cats extended their muscles, reaching a front paw ahead and a back leg out behind, then switched legs to get an all-around refreshing stretch before walking again. The felines started on their journey to the parking lot with the large boulders, backtracking on the same trail they had traveled all day. They were moving along at a good pace when Abby pointed out that they should be able to get back faster than it took to get here. "We won't have to stop to see the sights since we have already seen them." Oreo nodded in agreement, and together they trotted along. The two visited while still taking in the beauty of nature that surrounded them.

Oreo asked, "Are you enjoying your adventure?"

Abby responded quickly, "Yes, I am. This is really neat. There is so much to see, and it is so beautiful!"

The cats grinned, and then Oreo slowed his pace and softly said, "It wasn't very exciting for you, just going for a walk."

Abby got shoulder to shoulder with her new friend. "What do you mean *not exciting*? This is an amazing trip! I could not have dreamed up such an exploration. Besides, meeting you and getting to spend the day with you is what means the most to me."

Oreo stopped and looked at Abby, asking, "Really?"

"Of course," said Abby. "Making new friends is the best part of these adventures!"

Oreo said, "I see your point. I liked meeting you too!" With that, the cats continued on.

The two friends were making good time traveling down the now-familiar path as they made their way to their destination. They passed the platform and took a quick peek at the big waterfall. They crossed the bridge, and Abby said, "This is about halfway back, right?"

Oreo said, "That sounds about right."

The sun was heading toward the western sky, but there was still plenty of daylight left. The path began to narrow, and just before a sharp curve, it was only wide enough for one cat to walk at a time. The cats were quiet as Oreo led the way, with Abby right behind him. The black-and-white cat went around the curve and suddenly froze. Abby had to go off the path to not run into him.

"Oreo," Abby asked, "why did you stop?"

"Shhhhh," replied the cat. He looked back at his friend, and he had a frightened look on his face. He lifted his front paw and pointed down the path in front of them. He whispered, "Look. What is that *thing*?"

Even though he had spoken softly, Oreo's words carried through the woods, and the *thing* turned its head and looked directly at the felines. Abby murmured, "Whatever it is, it's alive!" A ball of black fur stood up on four stumpy legs, then up on its hind legs, sniffing the air. About twice the size of the cats, it had beady little eyes, rounded ears, and a pointy black nose at the end of a tan-colored muzzle. The startled cats stared, trying to figure out what they were seeing. Neither cat moved as they watched the animal drop back down on all fours. With its nose still in the air, sniffing, it started walking slowly toward the cats. The forest was eerily silent as the jet black creature got closer, and it stopped when the gap between the cats and the furry thing was about half of what it had been. Only a few seconds had passed when a loud roar came out of the black ball and resounded through the forest. The noise frightened both cats right off their feet, and after they landed (on their feet, of course) they bolted up the nearest tree. They ran so fast it almost seemed that they were spinning their wheels. Suddenly, there was another blast of the scary noise, only much louder! Out of the trees came a giant version of the black ball of fur, and it was running straight toward the tree that held the adventurous friends.

Abby and Oreo were high up in the tree. They looked down and saw that the smaller of the two creatures had followed the felines. It was holding on to the tree trunk, just a few limbs lower than where the cats were perched. Before the two cats could react, the bigger fur ball was at the base of the tree, then standing on its hind legs. It began to push on the tree, which made all of the branches shake! The frightened cats meowed, and the big beast stopped pushing against the tree. The tree became still, and the woods became very quiet. The bigger of the two roaring creatures surprised the cats when it started climbing the tree to where the smaller fur ball was still sitting. Oreo was the closest to the hairy beasts, and he summoned all his courage and turned to face them. He tried to be brave, puffing up his coat to appear bigger than he was, and growled, "You can climb trees… Are you some type of cat?"

Immediately, another roar blasted from the bigger of the two. The smaller one looked up at Oreo and asked. "What is a cat?"

Oreo looked surprised and replied, "We are cats. Aren't you one?"

The bigger creature climbed a bit higher on the tree trunk to look over the little one and, in the deepest voice either of the friends had ever heard, said, "We are black bears, and we live here. The woods is our home. What are you doing here?"

Abby knew she had to be strong and supportive for Oreo. She turned around on the branch to face the bears. "We came here on an adventure, a nature hike in this beautiful forest, but just for the day. You live here all the time?"

The little bear replied, "Yep! We are standing in our backyard! Where do you live?"

While the little bear and the two cats conversed, the bigger bear watched the interaction closely. Then in a growly voice, she said, "Come on, son, time for us to get down out of the tree." Using some very big claws for grip, the large ball of fur gracefully moved down until it was on the ground.

"Okay, Ma," said the little bear, and with his own claws, he duplicated the movement. Soon the two were standing on the earth near the base of the tree. The little bear looked up at the two cats and asked, "Are you coming down?"

Abby and Oreo looked at each other, then looked at the bigger bear, and then at each other again. They weren't too sure that coming down the tree would be a great idea. As he tapped the leg of the big bear, his little voice said, "Ah, gee, Ma, you scared the cats with your loud roars. You won't hurt my new friends, will ya?"

The big bear checked out her little cub to make sure he was okay, then looked up at the cats still sitting on the tree limb. "I have never seen a cat before. I didn't know if you were going to hurt my baby, so I roared to scare you away. I don't think you are going to hurt us now, and we won't hurt you. Come on down, and we can get to know one another a little better."

Oreo felt more comfortable after he heard the words that came from the two bears. He started down the tree, but Abby didn't follow. Once Oreo reached the earth, he turned around, expecting to see the long-tailed cat right behind him. Abby meowed softly as she contemplated how she was going to get down. She thought back to when she was a kitten, the day the Mr. rescued her from the tree when the neighbor's dog had wanted to play. Concerned, Oreo whispered to his friend, "What's the matter? Why aren't you coming down?"

Abby only meowed again and looked away. Oreo remembered their conversation on the platform, when Abby was so afraid of falling. He had started to speak up when the bigger bear interrupted. Although her voice was very deep, she spoke softly and asked, "Would you like some help getting down from the tree?"

Abby replied, "I feel like I am stuck up here."

Excitedly, the little bear began dancing about while talking to his mama. "Ma, remember when you had to help me get down the first few times I climbed trees? Ma, remember? Can you climb up and help the cat down just like you did me? Can ya, Ma?"

Gently patting her little one on the head with her massive paw, she answered, "Yes, Junior, I can help our new friend." As slick as a whistle, the big bear began a slow ascent up the tree trunk until she was face-to-face with the long-tailed cat. Abby was wide-eyed as she took in the size of the massive animal in front of her. The paw of the brute was bigger than the cat's head, and she contemplated what would happen next. The bear smiled and asked, "Do you think you can climb between me and the tree trunk? You can face me and hold on around my neck, and we will go down the tree together. This way, you won't be able to fall forward or backward and my arms will wrap around both sides of you like a basket." The nervous feline knew that she needed to trust this enormous creature to get to the ground. She accepted the offer with a quiet "Yes, thank you."

With one paw, Abby reached through the air until her white-tipped mitt landed on the torso of her rescuer. Gently the bear wrapped one of her immense front legs around and behind the kitty for support, until she found the security of the bear's chest. Abby wrapped her front legs around the bear's neck as far as she could reach and felt snug when the tree trunk shored up her backside. The hairy carrier posed the question to Abby if she was ready, and she said she was. Holding on tightly, she felt the strength of the beast as they gingerly descended the timber until they reached the base of the tree trunk. Tenderly the bear took Abby in her paws and set her on the ground next to Oreo.

Heaving a sigh of relief, the black cat looked at the big black bear. "Thank you so much for helping me."

"I was happy to help do it," said the bruin.

Junior was patting his mama's back, saying, "Good job, Ma, good job," and Oreo quietly asked Abby if she was all right. She nodded and gave her friend a slight smile.

The group of critters discussed the rescue for a bit, then Oreo said, "I guess we should officially introduce ourselves. My name is Oreo, and this beauty is my friend Abby." Simultaneously, the four smiled, and the smaller bear spoke up.

"It is nice to meet both of you. My name is Junior, and this is my mom, Mama Bear."

Abby spoke up and said, "Thank you again for helping me to get out of the tree. I don't know what I would have done if you hadn't been here."

With a little laugh, the bigger bear replied, "You probably wouldn't have run up the tree if I hadn't been here," then winked and chuckled a little more. Mama Bear told the cats, "I know we told you that we live here in the woods. When it is warm, we think of the entire woods as home and we roam all around. In the winter, we get a bunch of snow here. We plan for the change in the weather and we sleep the cold months away in a cozy den. Our coats are nice and thick to keep us warm."

Abby piped up, saying, "Your fur is very soft too. I was surprised when you held me up in the tree."

Oreo was looking at the bears' shape and size and said, "Hey, Junior, you don't have a tail."

The young bear replied, "What do you mean? I sure do—it is right here." The little bear wiggled his backside, and Oreo saw a little stub twitching. It made the cat laugh. Junior was laughing, too, and said, "Your tails are long—especially yours." He pointed at Abby, who made her appendage sway back and forth, saying, "That's what I've been told."

Oreo looked off to the western sky and knew the day's light was coming to an end. "New friends, I would love it if we could spend more time with you, but we have to get back to the parking lot before dark."

Junior asked, "Can we walk along with you for a while?"

"That is a great idea," said Abby. "We would like that!"

Mama bear stood up and said, "Would either of you want to ride on my back?"

The cats thought the offer from the big bear was very generous, and with a wink to each other, Abby said, "We would like that very much, if you really don't mind."

"Not at all." The big bear smiled, and she turned her side to the two friends. Oreo and Abby leaped up on the furry black ledge. Oreo sat down, but Abby started pumping her feet, one at a time, on the bear's back. The mama bear said, "Oh, that feels good. If you keep massaging me like that, I won't want to move!"

Abby chuckled and lay down to have the ride of a lifetime.

The animals shared a conversation about things they liked to do, comparing the activities. Suddenly, the big bear turned off the path and headed into the trees, with Junior following right behind her. Oreo sat up and timidly said, "Mama Bear, we need to get to the parking lot."

"Oh, I meant to tell you that I know a shortcut through the woods to get to the parking lot very quickly. We don't stay on the open path very often, so we know how to get around in the woods quite well. The parking lot is just over the hill in front of us. Going this way, we will get you there very soon."

Oreo relaxed and lay back down on the furry ride.

Both cats wanted to ask their new friends some questions. Junior and Mama Bear had questions of their own too. Looking up at the cats riding on his mother's back, Junior asked, "Can you tell us about where you live?"

Oreo replied, "I stay in a house not far from here with my Mrs. and her daughter."

Abby quickly added, "And I live with my own Mr. and Mrs.—a different Mrs. than the one Oreo lives with."

Mama Bear stopped suddenly, which caused her riders to slide off her furry back to the ground. She lay down on the ground and looked straight at the cats. "I am so sorry about that. Are you okay?"

Abby and Oreo both nodded, and Abby said, "We always land on our feet."

Mama Bear spoke up and muttered, "But…your Mr. and Mrs. are they *humans*?"

Hearing the word *humans*, Junior quickly went to his mother and crawled under her neck and sat between her big paws. Junior was trembling, and Mama Bear snuggled her son close, whispering that she would protect him.

"What's the matter?" asked Abby. "My Mr. and Mrs. are nothing to be afraid of."

Mama Bear asked again, "But are they humans?"

Abby replied, "They are people. I don't know what a human is."

Oreo sat down in front of their new friends. "Yes, Mama Bear, we live with humans, or people. They take care of us and love us just like you love Junior."

Mama Bear looked surprised, and Junior lay down, still nestled among his mother's front feet. Mama shook her head. "Other bears have told us that humans are mean to animals. My father told me that if I ever see one, I am to run the other way as fast as I can."

Abby was surprised. She said, "You would run from people? You are so big and strong! I am sure they would be more afraid of you than you are of them!" Abby went over next to Oreo, sat down, and asked, "Have either of you ever seen a person?" Mama shook her head no, while Junior hung his head in silence. Abby said, "What about you, Junior? Have you ever seen one?" Mama Bear nudged her little guy with her nose, and he whispered, "I saw some once." Mama Bear was surprised and raised herself up to a seated position, still hovering over her little one. In a parenting voice, she asked, "When did you see humans?"

Junior kept looking at the ground and was hesitant to tell the story, but he knew he had to share what they all wanted to hear. "Ma, remember when you went out to get some berries for us a while ago and you told me to stay in the den?" A drawn-out 'yyyyessss' came from the bigger bear. "I was bored and stuck my head out of the den, and I saw a little squirrel. I just had to chase it!"

The cats nodded in understanding, and Oreo said, "I just *love* to chase squirrels!"

Mama Bear gave Oreo a stern look, and the black-and-white cat sat down and looked away, still having a little grin on his face. Mama turned back to Junior, asking, "What happened next?"

Junior said, "I was on the way back to the den when I saw four humans, two big ones and two little ones. They were on the path."

Mama stood up and turned so she was in a position where she could look at her son and hear the rest of his story.

By now the cats had huddled together next to Mama Bear, all wrapped up in what the little bear was about to say. Abby spurted out, "That was probably a family—you know, a mom and a dad, and their children."

Oreo agreed, and Junior continued, "They didn't look scary, and they didn't see me. I ran up the nearest tree and just watched them as they walked along the path. The smallest one tripped on a little rock and fell down and started to cry. It was scared, and the biggest human picked up the little one and held it close until it stopped crying, just like Ma would do if I was scared…when I was little." The cats looked at each other and grinned.

Mama asked, "Were you scared?"

"No," said Junior. "I was just curious to see what they were and what they would do. They were different from anything I had ever seen, but I wasn't scared. They walked on down the path, and when they were out of sight, I climbed down from the tree and went back to the den."

Mama got down on her belly so she could look eye to eye with her son. Quietly she asked, "Why didn't you tell me about this?"

"I was afraid you would be mad that I left the den."

Mama Bear spoke very softly when she replied, "Junior, I am not mad. I am disappointed that you didn't obey me, and we will discuss that later, after we have seen our friends safely on their way. I don't tell you to stay in the den because I want to punish you. I am trying to protect you until I have a chance to teach you all you need to know to be out on your own. I love you very much and don't want anything to happen to you." Then the big bear wrapped her great big paws around her little one and hugged him tight while the cats cheered.

Oreo whispered to Abby, "We have all heard that before, haven't we?" Abby winked and smiled.

Mama Bear looked at the sun setting and said, "I hate to break this up, but I think we really need to get going."

Oreo said, "Mama Bear, can I say one more thing before we go?" Mama Bear looked at the black-and-white cat and nodded. Oreo went on, "People are like any other animals. They have families, and they try to teach their young right from wrong. There are good and bad cats, good and bad dogs, probably good and bad people. But most of the time, they are good and wouldn't hurt you or me."

Mama Bear said, "You are right, my friend. There are a few bad bears too. I shouldn't judge just because others have told me that all humans are mean. Thank you." With that, Oreo and the big bear both smiled.

Junior spoke up, saying, "Let's get the cats to the edge of the parking lot, Ma."

"Okay, little guy."

The group ventured up a hill. As they crested the mound, the cats were surprised to see the big rocks that lined the parking lot. They were back to their starting place.

Mama Bear stopped walking and spoke loud enough for all to hear. "This is as far as we should go."

The cats quit walking and looked at each other, then at the bears. "Gee, it was so nice to meet you and have this visit," said Abby.

Oreo said, "The entire day was great. The waterfall, the lake, but meeting our new friends today was the best part."

Mama Bear wrapped a paw around Junior and said, "Meeting you was wonderful for us too. Not only did we make new friends, but we also learned a valuable lesson: not to judge just by what others say. We can make up our own minds based on our own experiences."

Junior bobbed his head up and down, saying, "Yes, yes, yes!"

With that they said their goodbyes, and the mother and son turned and walked into the colorful woods, over the hill, and out of sight.

"Wow, that was really something," said Abby.

"It sure was," replied Oreo as the two cats headed for the bottomless box. When they reached the cardboard, Oreo looked at Abby and said, "I hate goodbyes, and I really need to get home, so I am going to leave first. Today was great, and I hope to see you again."

Abby smiled and started to reply, but Oreo turned his back and took off on a run through the parking lot and down the road. Abby stood for a moment, reflecting on the day before making her leap for home. Just before jumping into the box, she took a look back up the hill behind her. There, almost out of sight, sat Mama Bear and Junior. They smiled and waved at the pretty, long-tailed cat, and she waved back, then jumped headfirst into the portal to return home.

Abby was surprised when she woke up and realized she was in Mr.'s lap. "Well, hello, lovely," said the Mr. "You sure were in a deep sleep. The lady of the house was calling to you a couple of minutes ago. I think she has something for you." The man stroked the black cat gently, and she purred with affection, then pushed her head into his hand for more pampering. He scratched under her chin, and she purred louder. She was so content to be home in his lap. She was tired, and she quickly fell asleep again as he petted her.

Abby didn't know how long she had been asleep when she heard the Mrs. call her name. "Abby, Abby, come here, kitty. I have something for you." The cat yawned, lifted her head, and looked toward the kitchen.

"You better go see what she wants," said the Mr. and he picked up the soft-haired cat, gently set her on the floor, and she headed toward the kitchen. Again, the Mrs. called to her girl, and the kitty meowed softly as she stood by the lady's feet.

"There you are, my little girl." She bent down and picked up the cat, held her close, and gave her a little hug. Abby licked the Mrs. chin and nose, which she did quite often when she wanted the Mrs. to know that she was glad to see her. It always made the lady giggle, and Abby liked to see her happy. "I brought you something from the dentist's office today." Gently she put the cat on the floor. "The secretary's daughter was there, and she was selling some little stuffed animals to help raise money for her class trip with her school. They were so cute and little. I thought you might like to play with them." The Mrs. reached into the pocket of her apron and pulled out two tiny black stuffed animals. One was bigger than the other, and Abby came over to get a good look at the new toys. "Aren't they cute? They are little bears," said the Mrs., but she didn't have to tell the black cat. Abby was amazed at the coincidence of the bears she had met that day, and now she had toys that would always remind her of the friends in the woods. Abby gently picked the bears up with her mouth and ran with them to her cat tree in the corner of the living room. The cat tree had different platforms for the cat to sit on and had cubbyholes for the kitty to climb in—which cats like to do. Abby tucked the stuffed animals into one of the cubbyholes and whispered, "I will be back. You are safe here."

The long-tailed cat ran back to the kitchen and jumped up on the counter. She stroked the arm of her Mrs. to get her attention, and the Mrs. picked up her silky girl. Abby licked the lady's nose, chin, and cheeks with a lot of affection and enthusiasm. "Well, you must really like the bears!" Abby continued to lick her lady, and at the same time, her tail was swaying quickly back and forth. "I am glad you like them, but I have to cook dinner now." The Mrs. put Abby back on the counter. Abby jumped to the floor, then ran back to the cat tree, climbed into the cubby, and curled up around the bears, snuggling close. The excitement of the day found her again. She was still tired and very content. She curled herself around the new toys and went into a deep sleep.

After dinner, the Mr. and Mrs. looked in at Abby sleeping with her new toys. The Mrs. said, "She sure loves the toy bears. It is almost as if she is seeing old friends."

Chapter 4

Abby loved her life at the new house. She enjoyed watching the birds and squirrels and playing with the little stuffed bears that the Mrs. had brought to her the day of the adventure with Oreo. Not a day went by that the long-tailed cat did not reminisce on the trips with her friends. Abby had enjoyed the carnival, relished the spa treatment, and loved the forest, the waterfalls, and meeting Mama and Junior Bear. Occasionally she would give thought to what might be her next adventure and she would get a little excited, but then she would think of something else. She hadn't had the desire to go to the attic like she had on the days of her adventures.

One evening, Abby overheard the Mr. tell the Mrs. that he had to go out of town early the next week for a two-day conference with his boss. He had brochures of where the meeting would be, with lush golf courses and beautiful lakes. The man of the house sat down in his chair and was looking through the brochures when Abby jumped into his lap. While the Mr. stroked the soft fur of the black cat, he showed Abby the photos in the pamphlets. The pictures of the lakes and the parklike golf courses made Abby think of the spa trip with Toochee and the big lake she saw with Oreo.

The night before the Mr. left for his trip, Abby sat on the bed next to the suitcase as the man packed his clothes, books, and other items. Several times Abby would jump into the luggage. The Mr. would laugh and take her out, setting her next to the case on the bed. After the third time, he asked her to stay out of the bag so he could finish packing. The black cat lay down next to the case and watched him get ready for his trip. When he was done and was zipping the case shut, the Mr. told Abby that he would miss her while he was gone. He said that he would be home in a few days and she had to be a good kitty for the Mrs. He scratched her under her chin and rubbed her belly. In return, the silky cat purred loudly and stretched, hoping this moment would never end. That night, Abby slept curled up next to the Mr.'s legs on the big bed. She knew she would miss him while he was away.

A few days later, Abby woke up with the Mrs. when the alarm went off. The woman went down the stairs to the kitchen to start the day, while Abby jumped up on the sill of the bedroom window to look for birds at the feeder in the yard. The black cat sat there, watching the wild canaries, their yellow feathers so bold in the sunlight, as they fed on the seed that the lady of the house had put out for them. After a little while, the sleek feline padded down the stairs to see what the Mrs. was doing. She was just finishing up her breakfast. The Mrs. wished Abby a good morning, then picked the cat up and set her on the counter. The special lady stroked the black cat with affectionate rubs and asked her what she would like for breakfast. Abby looked up at her with her big green eyes. The Mrs. placed three cans of moist food on the counter and told Abby the flavors were chicken, tuna, or salmon. Abby put her white-tipped paw on the salmon and licked her lips. The Mrs. said, "Okay, my girl, you will get your favorite today," and she opened the can of salmon and spooned it into a pretty glass bowl. The woman placed the food in front of the cat and said, "Enjoy." Abby purred in delight and licked the lady's hand, showing her appreciation. The Mrs. told her kitty that the Mr. would be home by suppertime.

Abby was about two-thirds done with her delicious breakfast when the Mrs. came to tell her she was ready to go to work. As always, she gave the black cat lots of loving attention before leaving, then the woman headed out the door. Abby ran to the couch and looked out the window, watching the car go down the driveway and head out onto the road. The black cat was a little excited about the man of the house coming home and ran upstairs to lie on his bed to be a little closer to him. She ran past the spare room and went straight into the master bedroom. She jumped up on the bed and curled up on the Mr.'s pillow. She rolled her head on the pillow and was beginning to relax when suddenly she sat up straight, remembering that she had a dream the night before about an adventure.

The excitement kicked in, and the cat jumped off the bed and ran to the spare room. The long-tailed cat went through the doorway and was surprised when she noticed that the mirror door was partially open. She stood there, looking at the door, wondering when and why the Mr. or Mrs. had been up in the attic. Had they moved the bottomless box? Abby was more anxious than ever to get up there to see if the attic held any changes. She slid through the opening and ran up the stairs. When the long-tailed cat reached the top step, she stopped and looked around. Sunlight coming through the window lit the room. At first glance, Abby didn't notice anything different. She focused on the box and quickly went to the far end of the attic. Abby didn't want to think about not being able to go on any more adventures if the box was gone. She was relieved to see the magical cardboard square and sat down to catch her breath.

It wasn't long before the urge to travel got the black kitty back on her feet. Abby wondered about the day's adventure. She uttered aloud, "I won't find out until I jump!"

Suddenly, the attic vanished and the long-tailed cat was gently falling to an unknown destination. The soft landing was just like before, with the familiar puff of smoke that gave it a sense of magic. Abby inched her head out of the box to get a glimpse of her surroundings. The black cat and the bottomless box were sitting in some tall grass, hidden from sight. Before Abby jumped out of the box, she looked all around, and right behind her was a very large red building. Abby could see nothing but fields in every other direction. Some with plants in them, and others with animals grazing on grass, with big trees here and there. The sky was clear and blue and looked like it stretched for a million miles. Woods bordered the far edge of some of the fields. The groups of trees were so distant that they looked very tiny. Abby wondered if there were bears in the forest like there had been when she met Oreo and hiked on the nature trail. The planted fields looked familiar, and Abby realized they reminded her of the garden her family had last summer at the old house, when Abby was just a little kitten. The Mr. and Mrs. had grown corn, tomatoes, green beans, and some other vegetables. When the vegetables were ripe, the Mrs. had taken time off from work, and she stayed home to cook them and store them in canning jars to eat over the winter. Abby liked

it when the Mrs. was home all day with her. The silky cat got extra attention on those days, and she tried to show her love by trying to help the lady of the house when she worked in the kitchen. A slight breeze caused the tall grass to stir, and brought the kitty's thoughts back to the present.

Slowly Abby climbed out of the box. She walked along in the tall grass, keeping close to the red building. She finally reached the edge of the building, and she peeked over the grass, where she saw a big white house. The house had a wraparound porch that was shaded by the roof's overhang. Chairs on the porch were welcoming for family or friends, and a railing extended along the full length of the front of the house, almost like its own picket fence. A man and a woman sat in two of the chairs on the porch, a small table separating them. Abby felt a little tug at her heart as she thought about her own Mr. and Mrs. at home. Suddenly she felt a tap on her shoulder. It startled her, and she jumped straight up into the air. She looked behind her as she landed, and there was a cat sitting in the grass, soaking up the sunshine and grinning.

At first, Abby thought it was Tiger, as the fur was similar in color and had many of the same markings. Abby was excited and had turned quickly to greet her old friend when she realized this cat wasn't nearly as big as the friend she met at the carnival. It also had four white stockings and paws. Abby backed up a couple of steps because this cat didn't say anything or react in any way but the smile. Abby didn't know what to think, so she turned and ran quickly toward the back of the big red building and the comfort of the bottomless box. The other cat ran after her and was gaining on the black cat. It meowed loudly, "Wait, wait! Who are you?" Abby ran faster, but as she rounded the corner to the back of the barn, the other cat had caught up to her. The tiger-striped cat said, "Where did you come from?"

Abby realized that this must be the new friend for this adventure, so she turned around and sat down. The gray-striped cat sat down too. With a sweet little voice, the striped cat said, "I'm Ally Cat, and I have been staying here on this farm for a little while." Excitedly, the cat continued, "I am glad to have another cat here. Where did you come from?"

Abby replied, "Hi, Ally Cat. My name is Abby, and I came here on an adventure, but I don't know what a farm is. Can you tell me?"

Ally looked at Abby and said, "From what I can tell, a farm is a place where people grow food and have cows to get milk, and they share it with other people. There are different buildings and machinery to help with all of the work they have to do."

Abby looked wide-eyed as she took it all in, then said, "This is really terrific. I bet you like living here."

Ally said, "I had been lost and really didn't have a place to live. I happened to come across the field behind the barn. The man who lives here saw me and took me up to the house, where the lady gave me some tuna fish to eat and cream to drink. They have been so nice to me."

Abby thought about Oreo being at the shelter. Ally changed the subject and said, "Now it's my turn to ask you where you came from. You seemed to appear out of nowhere. Did you come across the back field too?"

Abby looked in the direction of her cardboard portal, then back at Ally. Abby realized that Ally hadn't said anything about having a dream of her own to meet her, so she decided to wait a little while to tell Ally the story of the magical portal. Instead, Abby smiled at Ally and said, "Let's look around."

The two felines started walking and followed the long side of the big red building, then went around a corner. They came to a huge door that was set on rollers, sliding to open and close. Currently, the entrance was open, and Ally led the way inside the building. A cement apron was the welcome mat to the building, and the floor in the barn was cement too. The shaded floor inside the barn was cool to the pads of the cat's paws. It was darker inside the barn, and it took a moment for the cat's eyes to adjust. Ally went about halfway into the building, then stopped as she waited for Abby to come up beside her. "The farm is what the family does for their job. This building is where Mr. Farmer keeps his machinery and tools. See the tractors?" The two cats walked farther into the building and saw several pieces of farm machinery. Ally continued, "He uses the equipment to plant and harvest crops in the fields. He sells some of what he grows and uses some to feed the animals here. There are milking cows, chickens for eggs, and horses that they ride when they find time. The cows here spend most of their time in the field, but they come to another barn twice a day to get milked." She smiled. "Come on," said Ally. "Let's go back outside, and I can show you some cows and horses."

The felines left the big barn through the same door they went in. As soon as they were out of the building, Ally pointed to a field and said, "There they are." Abby looked in the direction of the her friend's paw and saw a big field of grass with several cows and horses. The cows were black-and-white, and there were big ones and little ones. Standing near a few of the big cows was a little black horse munching on the lush green blades of grass. Bigger horses were spread about the pasture. Most of them were a reddish brown, but Abby also saw one that was a golden color. Abby looked at Ally and asked, "Why are there so many different sizes of these farm animals?"

Ally faced her new friend and replied, "The big cows are grown-up, and the little ones are their babies. Mr. Farmer likes that because the herd gets larger when they have babies. They grow really fast." Abby was amazed as she took in the information. "The horses, they are all grown up but are different kinds. The little black one is a pony, and ponies are smaller horses. The other horses are the size of most horses that people use for riding." Ally pointed at a wooden structure in the field. "See that building? That is where the horses sleep and where Mrs. Farmer keeps all the equipment she needs to care for them. Just past there is the milking parlor, where the cows go to give their milk. The milk is stored in a cooler until a big truck comes, picks it up and takes it to the stores to sell. Come on, I will show you the chickens and rabbits." Ally led the way to the far side of the barn. Along the side of the barn, there were a few raised boxes with sides and bottoms of chicken wire. Past those boxes was a little shed up against the barn, and it was surrounded on three sides by a wire fence. Inside the fence were chickens and chicks scratching around in the dirt. The two cats walked closer and came to the small boxes, which were elevated off the ground. Abby could see that there was a bunny rabbit in each box. She kept walking to the fence so she could see all the chickens. Ally had stopped by the rabbit cage and was busy watching an ant cross in the dirt in front of her.

Abby looked back and saw Ally concentrating on something and went over beside her new friend to watch too. The two cats stared at the ant, following it with their eyes. Nothing moved on the cats but the tips of their tails twitching back and forth. One of the chickens squawked and interrupted their trance. The cats looked at each other, and they both laughed. Abby wanted to know more about the rabbits and the chickens. She was just about to ask about them when Ally yelled, "Get to a tree, *now!*" and the farm cat took off running to the nearest tree. Up she went, and she didn't come to a stop until she was on the first appendage, about six feet from the ground. The long-tailed black cat followed Ally's lead. When they both were seated on the limb, Abby recognized a noise coming from the base of their perch. Looking down, she saw a big golden colored dog staring back at her and barking nonstop. The black cat felt her heart racing, and she looked at Ally, who shook her head and said, "I should have warned you about Buster. He lives down the road. He was here yesterday and chased me up this tree then too."

Abby had caught her breath, and she looked down again at the canine. The dog was focused on the two cats and still barking. Abby asked, "How long will he stay there?"

Ally grinned. "Not too long, because the farmers don't like to hear the barking. As long as they are home, either Mr. or Mrs. Farmer will come out and send him on his way."

As if the farmer had heard Ally, he came out of the house and gave a big shout. "Buster, go home!" The dog paid no attention and continued yapping. Coming down from the porch, the farmer headed toward the hound, muttering all the way. When Mr. Farmer got close, he snarled at the pooch to take off. Buster quit barking but maintained an unbroken stare into the tree and was wagging his tail. The farmer looked up the tree and was surprised to see two cats perched on a branch—one he had never seen before. "Well, hello, kitties. All of a sudden, there are two of you!"

Abby twitched her tail, and Ally gave her a little grin. The farmer looked at Buster and stomped his foot at the dog. "You go on home now," he said and stomped his foot again. Buster followed the command and headed off through the yard in the direction of his residence. Mr. Farmer looked up at the cats and, with a big smile, said, "The two of you are safe and can come down now. Buster is gone. I will go tell Mrs. Farmer that another cat has come to call. Come on up to the porch. I bet we can find some fresh cream for the two of you."

Abby didn't move, but Ally trusted the man who was walking toward his house, so she started down the tree. Abby tried to follow Ally, but when she thought about climbing down, she had the familiar feeling of being stuck. It was a long way to jump, and she wasn't sure she could do it without getting hurt, if she could summon the courage to make such a leap. Ally had gotten to the ground, and the farmer was halfway to the porch steps when Abby meowed in frustration, wondering how to get down. The farmer stopped walking when he heard the woes of a cat. He turned around and could see that the black cat might need some help. Ally was at the base of the tree, looking up at her friend, and smiled to herself when the farmer approached her. He reached up and gently lifted the long-tailed cat off the branch, and Abby softly meowed in thanks. He brought the black cat to his chest and stroked her head. Purrs of appreciation came from Abby, and as he stroked her fur, he said, "You sure have a soft coat. Ma would love to pet you." Abby nudged his hand, and he patted her head before setting her down next to Ally. "Let's go get that snack." Mr. Farmer again ventured toward the house, and Ally trotted that way, too, with Abby right behind her.

Shortly before the man arrived at the porch, he looked to the side of the house and he gave a wave at two people that were standing by a tall post in the yard. One had a midsize yellow ball in hand. The farmer shouted, "You girls having fun?"

The girl with the ball replied, "We sure are! We are going to play a game of tetherball. Want to join us?" The second girl smiled and nodded in agreement.

Chuckling, the farmer replied, "Maybe later. Right now I have to find some goodies for these two cats."

The girls ran over and stopped when they got close to the porch. They both sat down on the ground and called, "Here, kitty, kitty." The two felines went to the girls, who started petting them and saying all kinds of sweet words to the fur babies. The farmer looked down at the girls pampering the cats and said, "I will go in and see if I can find some snacks." The girls continued fussing over the cats, who purred loudly in appreciation.

When the farmer got inside the house, he called out, "Honey, come see what I found."

The farmer's wife came out of the kitchen, asking, "What is it?" The man pointed out the screen door. "Oh my, another one? Two kitties in just a few weeks!" The man suggested they take some refreshments outside for the cats, for the girls, and for themselves. The two people disappeared into the kitchen, and a few minutes later, they headed for the door, each carrying a tray loaded with goodies. Once they were out on the porch, they set the trays on the table between the chairs and asked who was thirsty. The girls and the felines hurried up the porch steps to see the offering. Iced tea and pie for the girls and the farmers. For the cats, ground turkey and fresh milk. While she ate, Abby could hear bits and pieces of what the people discussed. First, the conversation was about the girls and the game they were playing, then moved on to the two cats showing up at their farm. Mr. Farmer told the others how the neighbor's dog had the cats up the maple tree by the mailbox and that was when he first saw the black cat. Mrs. Farmer said, "I don't think I have seen either of these cats around here before. We will have to listen to the radio and call the shelter to see if someone is looking for them." The woman said she was going to call the local veterinarian too. She felt certain someone would be looking for their pets.

The lady wanted to get a good look at Abby. She bent down and stroked the cat's head and back. "What a soft kitty you are, and you have such a long tail!" Abby purred loudly in appreciation.

"Listen to that motor," said the farmer. "She sounds like my tractor!"

Ally came over and nudged the woman's hand, as she wanted to be petted too. Mrs. Farmer reached around Abby to pet Ally, then started using both hands to caress both cats at the same time.

Abby and Ally had licked their bowls clean. Purring, they wound themselves around the people's legs, saying thank-you in their own way. With a smile in her voice, the farmer's wife said, "Okay, kitties, I need to get back to my chores in the kitchen. I won't get my housework done if I stay out here with you." She stroked both the cats from head to tail with loving affection. "You should get back to work too, Sweetie," and the lady gave her husband a kiss on the cheek. Mr. Farmer grinned, then headed for the barn. The girls helped Mrs. Farmer take the dishes inside the house. The cats sat on the porch and watched as the people all went on their way. Ally walked over the where the top step met the porch, and lay down. There was a ray of sunshine coming through the trees right to the spot where she was, making it nice and warm. She said,

"I'm ready for a nap," and she put her head on her paws. Abby thought that a nap sounded like a good idea. The long-tailed cat chose one of the cushioned chairs for her resting spot, and once she was in the chair, she curled up like cats do. It wasn't long before both cats were sleeping soundly.

Abby woke up when she heard a thump, then another thump. She opened her eyes and saw that Ally was awake and was sitting on one of the porch steps. Abby stood up, had a big stretch, and then joined her new friend. Ally was watching the two girls. They were in the yard beside the house. Between the girls was a tall thin pole. One end of a rope was tied to the top of the pole, and the other end of the rope was tied to the yellow ball that one of the girls was holding earlier. The ball hung about halfway down the pole. The cats watched as one girl would swat the ball to the left or right of the pole, and it became a target for the other player to slap it back to the first player. The girls laughed as they hit the ball back and forth to each other. When they hit the ball, it made the thumping sound that woke Abby. The long-tailed cat said, "Wow! That would be a perfect game for cats if it were smaller." Ally started to laugh as she gave that some thought. The cats continued to watch the two girls play, and Abby started thinking about getting back home. She looked at Ally and said, "Earlier today, you asked me where I came from. I think it is time I told you." Ally looked at her friend with curiosity. Abby said, "Let's walk to the back of the barn while we talk." Abby started down the steps, and Ally was right behind her.

The two cats padded across the yard, and before long, they were behind the barn. Abby took a quick glimpse toward the long grass, where she had left her transportation. She breathed a little sigh of relief to see that the bottomless box was still there next to the building. Abby said, "I came to the farm in that box," and she pointed toward the cardboard.

Ally said, "What do you mean?"

The two cats continued walking, and Abby began to tell the story of how she had a dream that led her to that cardboard box. Abby was about to tell of her leap of faith when she heard a motor. She stopped talking and looked toward the noise. She saw Mr. Farmer on a small machine with four wheels. He was on the riding lawn mower, cutting the grass. He had been mowing on the side of the barn by the chicken and rabbit pens. He headed toward the back of the barn to turn the mower around. He smiled when he saw the cats in the tall grass and noticed they were near a cardboard box.

Suddenly, memorable barking filled the air and was much too close. "It's Buster!" screamed Ally, just as the big dog came around the corner of the barn, headed straight for them. The farmer saw the dog, too, and looked around, hoping the cats could get to a high spot before Buster caught up with them. Mr. Farmer jumped off the tractor, and he ran toward the cats and hollered gruffly in an attempt to stop the dog's pursuit.

Without thinking, Abby ran to the safest place she knew. She got to the bottomless box and leaped in, beginning her gentle free fall home. As she floated through the portal, everything that had just happened was going through her mind. She was concerned as she wondered what would become of Ally with that dog chasing her. Back behind the barn, the farmer had tried to scare Buster off, but the dog had gotten to the spot where the box had been and was whining as he sniffed the grass. Mr. Farmer ran up to the dog and told him to go home. Once the dog was out of sight, the farmer looked for the cats and the box that they had jumped into, but there was nothing there. He had expected that he would need to calm the cats down after the terrorizing ordeal and was shocked when the box and the cats had disappeared! "What? Where? What happened to the cats?" he questioned. He brushed the grass and looked all around. He had only taken his eyes off the box and the cats for just a few seconds when he heard Buster barking, and now they were gone. This was a mystery he couldn't explain, and he headed for the house to tell Mrs. Farmer what had happened.

Abby awoke on the bed in the master bedroom. She lifted her head and found comfort in the familiar surroundings. Her memory took her back to the farm, where she had met another friend and had such a fun day. She was saddened that she didn't get to say goodbye to her new friend, and she hoped Ally was able to get away from the neighborhood dog. She sat up and stretched while she looked around the room. There was the Mr.'s exercise bicycle, and the Mrs.' dressing table. Abby could see herself in the mirror above the table, and she noticed that there was something on the bed behind her. She turned around and gasped when she realized it was Ally! Her farm friend was curled up nose to tail, sleeping soundly. Abby couldn't believe her eyes. She licked her front paw and rubbed her face, shook her head, and looked again. Abby remembered that Ally had been right behind her when Buster was chasing them. When she jumped in the box for safety, Ally must have jumped in too. Abby gave this a lot of thought while Ally was still asleep, lying there next to the Mr.'s pillow.

Abby moved gently until she was right next to her friend and softly tapped the sleeping kitty on the shoulder. "Ally, wake up," she whispered. "Ally, it's me, Abby. Please wake up."

Ally stirred, opened her eyes, and stretched, one leg at a time, followed by arching her back high. Ally smiled when she saw Abby, then her eyes grew wide as she realized she was in a room where she had never been before. "Where…where are we?" she asked.

Abby said, "Don't worry. You are safe. You are at my home."

Ally jumped off the bed and looked around. "How did we get here?"

Abby grinned and replied, "The same way I got to the farm—magically!"

Ally looked at her friend, and she was completely confused.

"Follow me and I will explain everything."

Abby started walking to the spare bedroom and the mirrored door that led the way to the attic. Without hesitation, Ally followed the long-tailed cat. Soon the two friends stood in front of the looking glass. Abby pushed the magnet on the bottom corner of the mirror, and the door swung open. The black cat went through the doorway and headed up the stairs. The farm cat glanced behind her before following her friend into the darkened stairwell and up the steps that led to the attic. As before, sunshine flowed through the windowpanes, illuminating the room. Abby sat down and began to divulge to Ally the events that led to their meeting at the farm. She started with the move to this house, the dreams of adventures, the desire to come to the attic, and finding the cardboard box. Ally sat in silence, amazed as Abby shared her stories. She told of the carnival and her new friend Tiger, the spa and meeting Toochee, and then about the nature trail in the woods with Oreo. Abby mentioned that all the new friends had said that they had dreams, too, about meeting a new friend. Continuing, the black cat shared how the last trip through the portal took her to the farm. The sleek black cat watched the expressions on Ally's face as she listened in amazement.

Suddenly, Ally looked at Abby and said, "I had a dream too! It was the night before you got to the farm. I had fallen asleep on a soft pile of hay in the barn. I was dreaming that I was going to see a black cat and go on a magical journey… Oh my, the cat in my dream, her name was Abby, and she had a long tail! It was *you!*" Excitement stirred between the two of them.

Abby said, "Our meeting was meant to be! Isn't it exciting?"

Ally nodded, and the two kitties frolicked around the attic with the joy of friendship. Then, apparently anxious, Ally stopped in her tracks and stammered, "What will happen to me? How will I get back to the farm?"

Abby sat down and looked at her buddy. She was thinking about the dilemma they faced, and then her eyes twinkled and a smile emerged. "Maybe the question is this: Do you really want to go back to the farm?"

Ally cocked her head, not sure she understood what her friend was saying. Before she replied, Abby said, "You told me that you had been staying at the farm after being lost, but you didn't say it was your home. Would you like to stay here with me?"

Ally was almost afraid to hope. "Do you think I could?"

The hostess bobbed her head up and down and said, "I think so. Before my first adventure, I overheard the Mr. and Mrs. talking about getting another cat to keep me company, and here you are! All we have to do is figure out how we introduce you to my Mr. and Mrs. They are going to wonder how you got into the house."

As if on cue, a woman's voice was heard calling from downstairs. "Abby, my little girl, where are you?"

Abby and Ally looked at each other. They were both wondering how the next few minutes were going to go. "Abby, come here, girl." Abby knew the time had come for her new friend and her family to meet.

"Let's go downstairs, but stay behind me, out of sight, for a little bit." Ally agreed, and they ventured down the attic stairs. When they got to the spare bedroom, they started for the main floor when they heard a lady's voice as the Mrs. called again.

"Kitty, kitty, I brought you something today. Come see what it is."

The silky black cat had entered the hallway with her new friend right behind her. Abby came to an abrupt stop and turned around. She whispered, "Wait here," and she ran past her friend and into the spare room. From the hallway, Ally watched Abby go to the attic door and gently push it until the click of the magnet confirmed that the door had closed. "There," said Abby. "We can't leave any sign of us going to the attic." Ally nodded as Abby passed by her in the hallway, and the two cats headed down the stairs and into the living room. The newcomer slowed and stayed back a bit, making sure she was out of sight behind the recliner while Abby headed for the kitchen.

"Hello, pretty girl," said the lady of the house. She bent down and picked up the black cat, petting her head affectionately. Abby pushed her head into her lady's hand and purred loudly, enjoying the caresses. For a moment, she forgot about Ally being there. The Mrs. gently set the black cat on the kitchen floor. As she did, she stroked her back all the way to the tip of her long tail and said, "I have a new toy for you." Then the Mrs. grabbed a large paper bag from the kitchen table and headed for the living room. Abby followed her and watched as the Mrs. sat down on the floor, reached into the bag, and pulled out a package. Abby looked beyond the Mrs. and saw Ally. She was peeking around the chair, watching the owner of the house give a gift to her pet. The Mrs. was looking at the package, turning it over and reading some writing on the wrapper. Abby had lost interest and jumped into the empty paper bag. "You silly cat, that bag isn't your toy!" Abby tried to jump out of the paper enclosure, but the bag fell over onto its side. Abby lay down in the toppled bag and watched the Mrs. take the items out of the package and start assembling the gift.

"Oh, kitty, I think you are going to love this!"

Abby focused on the lady as she looked at all the different pieces that had been in the bag and now sat on the floor in front of her. The woman held up a piece of wood about the size of the couch pillows, but it was flat and thin. The wood was light in color and had a small hole in the center. The underside of the board was weighted and was much heavier than it appeared, and the lady placed the board on the floor beside her. Next, the Mrs. picked up a thin brass rod that was about as long as the paper bag that Abby was in. The top of the rod had a small swivel with a hole in its center. Abby watched as the woman picked up a thin yellow cord and put one end of the cord through the eye of the swivel, then tied it tightly into a knot. The cord was about half the length of the rod. Abby rushed out of the paper bag and tried to grab the loose end of the cord. The Mrs. pulled the cord back and said, "Not yet, little one, but it won't be long."

The woman picked up a small ball. The ball was the same color as the cord, and it had a small tab at the top, which had a hole in the center. The Mrs. took the free end of the cord and began to thread it through the hole on the tab of the ball. Abby stared as she realized that this toy looked familiar. It was just like the tetherball game that the girls were playing at the farm! Abby started nudging the woman while she tried to get the cord tied to the ball.

"Goodness, Abby, you sure seem excited!"

When the ball was finally secured on the cord, the lady of the house placed the rod upright into the hole in the board. The rod was secured as it was twisted in the wood until it was tight. The Mrs. started to explain to her long-tailed cat that she would be able to bat the ball and it would swing around to her to bat it again. The lady gave the ball a gentle swing, and the ball circled around to Abby, who got on her hind legs and gave it a good swat with one of her paws. The Mrs. giggled with delight as she watched her black cat's happy reaction to the toy. Her giggle went to a gasp when another cat came running from behind the recliner and rushed at the toy! The woman sat in shock as the second cat stopped at one side of the toy and batted the yellow ball back to Abby, who was on the other side. The Mrs. watched the two cats play the game, taking turns swatting the ball to each other. The woman studied the new kitty. It looked like a tiger cat but had four white stockings for paws. The striped cat wasn't as big as Abby but was very competitive at the game the cats were playing. A couple of minutes had passed when Abby caught sight of the woman sitting on the floor staring at Ally. Abby stopped playing and walked toward her lady. As the ball stopped swinging, Ally watched Abby and slowly followed her friend.

The Mrs. leaned back against the couch and watched as the cats approached her. Abby arrived first, and the lady's hand stroked the black cat's head with affection. Ally, unafraid, boldly stepped up on the woman's lap and faced her host. The Mrs. was smiling, and with her other hand, she petted the unexpected guest lightly on her

head. Speaking softly, she said, "Hello, there, pretty kitty. Where did you come from?" The Mrs. noticed the cat had the marking of a heart in her fur on her forehead. Ally pressed her head in the palm of the petting hand, and both cats were purring with appreciation with the lady's reaction to the situation.

"Abby, is this your friend?"

Abby stepped closer and began to lick the back of the woman's hand, hoping that her action would be a response that was understood. The lady reached under Ally, picked her up, and brought the cat into her chest. She snuggled her and told her how soft her belly fur was and how she liked her booties. She talked softly to the cat in her arms and to the black cat, who was now sitting next to her. "I bet the two of you would like something special to eat!" The cats seemed to understand her.

Ally stepped out of the Mrs. arms, and Abby whispered, "Come with me!" and both felines headed for the kitchen.

The woman rose to her feet and said, "Wait for me, you two," and grinned from ear to ear as she followed the two cats. She went to the cupboard and pulled out a can of tuna fish. She opened the tin and spooned its contents into two bowls. Setting the bowls on the floor in front of the furry friends, she smiled as they began eating without hesitation. While the cats were enjoying their feast, she started to think about where this second cat came from.

The Mrs. picked up the phone and called the local animal shelter. She described their guest, but the shelter workers hadn't heard of any missing cats that looked like that. The caring woman called her neighbors, but they didn't know of anyone that had a cat like Abby's friend. Next, she dialed the veterinarian's office and had the same results—they didn't know anyone missing a cat that looked like the one that the Mrs. described. She made an appointment for the new cat to see their animal doctor to make sure the kitty was healthy. The Mrs. asked all the people she spoke with to let her know if anyone called about a missing cat. She was hoping no one would claim the fuzzy-pawed cat, as Ally had already claimed her heart.

Just as the Mrs. hung up the phone, the Mr. came home from his trip and walked into the kitchen. The Mrs. greeted him with a smile and a hug, then told him she had a real surprise for him. She looked around the kitchen, but the cats were no longer in sight. The couple stepped into the living room, and the Mrs. pointed to the Mr.'s recliner, where the two furry friends were curled up together and both were sound asleep.

The Mr. looked at the two cats and then at his wife in surprise. She smiled and told the story of how she discovered Abby's friend in the house, the calls she made, and feeding them the tuna fish. She stated that she hadn't figured out how the new cat got into their house. The Mr. reminded the Mrs. that the new house had a pet access door in the entryway. They decided that had to be the answer. The Mr. walked over to the recliner and gave the guest a gentle stroke on her back. Both cats stirred, and Ally picked up her head to acknowledge the attention from the man of the house. He said hello to the striped cat and gently picked her up, holding her close in his arms while Abby watched the interaction. The cat brushed her head against the man's arm while he gave her some loving attention. She reacted with a roly-poly sound, as if she was humming a tune amid the purring. He looked at the Mrs. and asked her if she had given her a name. She responded that she hadn't had time to think about it.

He said, "Well, if she was a stray, we could call her Ally, like an alley cat."

Abby and Ally looked at each other with wide eyes and heard the Mrs. tell her husband that name was perfect. Ally would be the name of the new cat. He set the cat back on the recliner next to Abby, and the two cats snuggled together. The Mr. squatted down in front of the two felines and said, "Ally, welcome to our family. The Mrs. and I are thrilled that you are here, and you seem to be friends already with our long-tailed kitty. I bet that you and Abby will have many fun adventures."

Abby winked at her new friend and thought to herself, *I bet we will too. All we have to do is DREAM!*

About the Author

Shirley M. Young lives in the Upper Peninsula of Michigan, a serene area filled with nature. Encompassed by the Great Lakes, her home is amid many inland lakes, thousands of acres of forest, waterfalls, and abundant wildlife. Shirley M. Young has enjoyed writing since she was a child. Publications include magazine articles and, for several years, a popular weekly column for a local paper. Writing is a way to relax in her downtime following a full-time job and a consistent exercise program, usually being at the gym by 5:00 a.m.

She and her husband of thirty-four years have two adult sons and one grandson, also residing in Michigan. At home, two tabbies and a happy yellow lab fill the house with love and laughter. A choir member and deacon of her church, Shirley also is a substitute Sunday school teacher. Spending time with all those she loves, making crafts, playing cards and board games, fishing, and having long walks through the woods are the things that she enjoys.

CPSIA information can be obtained
at www.ICGtesting.com
Printed in the USA
LVHW071543160421
684723LV00048B/1732